The Luck of the
MISS L.

The Luck of the
MISS L.

Lee Kingman

Houghton Mifflin Company
Boston   1986

Library of Congress Cataloging-in-Publication Data

Kingman, Lee.
  The luck of the Miss L.

  Summary: Eleven-year-old Alec's dream of winning an
upcoming rowing race is endangered when a near-fatal
boating accident shakes his confidence.
  [1. Boats and boating—Fiction. 2. Rowing—Fiction.
3. Self-confidence—Fiction] I. Title.
PZ7.K595Lu 1986   [Fic]   85-27507
  ISBN 0-395-40421-5

Printed in the United States of America

P   10 9 8 7 6 5 4 3 2 1

For Lydia Eeva
May she discover the fun of
boats and rowing!

1

Alec checked his watch. The digits winked. Another minute gone, but . . . so . . . slowly. He slipped the watch off his wrist and shook it, as if he could speed up time by jiggling it. It still read 8:51. He stared at it until it winked: 8:52. He put it back on his wrist. It worked all right. In a few minutes he'd know if number 1924, 1925, 1926, 1927, or 1928 would be his lucky number. His lucky summer. His lucky boat — the first prize of the raffle.

Where had he put his ticket stubs? Not in his pants pocket! Panic! until he tapped his other pants pocket. A whew of relief. He palmed the stubs in his hand so he could rush for his prize when Miss Teen Annisconset reached into the painted wooden sea chest with the authentic rope handles (the third prize) which held all the tickets deposited for the raffle of prizes at the annual Sea Fest. Alec had waited until 8:40 P.M. to buy his chances from Mrs. Pinkham, who was presiding over the raffle table.

"Taking a last-minute number?" she had asked.

"No. I've been waiting all day so my numbers won't

be at the bottom. And I want five tickets." He had
handed over four dollar bills and four quarters and
printed his name, Alexander Mott, address, and phone
number so carefully onto each ticket that his were the
last ones to go in. At 8:45 Mrs. Pinkham had closed
the lid of the chest and sent Mr. Keebler to look for
Miss Teen Annisconset. The drawing for prizes would
be the high point and wind-up of the summer fair.

*

Alec knew Miss Teen Annisconset. She was Linda
Buker, who had had braces on her teeth when she
baby-sat for his little sister two summers ago. Alec had
called her Metalmouth and she had called him Smart-
ass — or Smartalec when his parents were around. He
wished they had been on better terms. If she knew who
held numbers 1924 through 1928, she wouldn't call
them. She didn't like him. She'd complained about
him all the time: "Mrs. Mott, Jeannie's stroller won't
push. Alec bent the wheels." (Alec had tried to borrow the wheels for a project, but he found he couldn't
get them off without using such force that replacing
them would be no secret.) Or, "Mrs. Mott, Jeannie's
crying so hard I can't get her to stop. Alec poked her
again." Alec had only tickled her to make her let go
of his comic book. He knew better than to poke
Jeannie.

But Linda had been crowned winner of the Sea
Fest's Miss Teen Pageant. "If you can call fifteen girls
sweating in bikinis on the front porch of the Town
Hall at high noon a pageant!" Alec had heard his

2

mother say. Now Linda's smile shone not from braces on her teeth but from the same kind of glossy stuff on her lips that Jeannie liked to fool around with when she played dress up.

*

As Mr. Keebler ushered Miss Teen Annisconset onto the porch, Alec thought Linda's lips were so shiny that her smile would gleam in the dark without her. He ducked behind a pillar of the porch and began chanting in his head: 1924, 1925, 1926, 1927, 1928. Come on, Linda! Put your hand in and pull out one of those numbers. For the dinghy. I don't want the second prize — that painting. I don't want any of the fourth prizes — that crocheted blanket thing or the other junk. Not even the sea chest. It's the boat. The dinghy. The skiff. Whatever you call it, it floats. The oars come with it. Please, please, God. Please, please, Linda Buker, Miss Teen Annisconset. You have to give me that boat!

Mr. Keebler adjusted the standup mike for the PA system and rumbled into it. His words disappeared under the throb of music being fed into the system by the DJ in charge of tapes. "Squ-AWK!" said Mr. Keebler. "SQUU-awk that music!" Then in the sudden silence his voice blotched out into the air. "Your attention please FOLKS. Gather round. This is the BIG event — the drawing for the FAB-U-lous prizes so generously donated by the GOOD PEE-pul and MERchants of Annisconset. Now, how shall we do this, start with the fourth prizes and work up to first?"

3

"Certainly," said Mrs. Pinkham. "If two of you strong boys will just lift this chest up onto the porch and set it down on that bench, then Miss Annisconset can stand right here —" Alec knew Mrs. Pinkham could stage-manage anything from a play about tooth decay to a fire drill. Four years ago, when the Motts had moved to Annisconset from Indiana, she had been his third grade teacher.

While Mrs. Pinkham was organizing the prize drawing, Alec looked out at the gathering crowd. There was his mother. She'd taken two tickets because she wanted both the oil painting and the sea chest. There was his father carrying Jeannie on his shoulders. He didn't believe in raffles. "Just figure the mathematics out and you'll know it's a bummer," he advised Alec. "Save your money and eventually you can buy a boat."

"Have you done the math on that?" Alec had asked. "If I didn't do *anything* — didn't spend any money at all — if I saved my two-fifty-a-week allowance I'd be through school before I got a boat! I'd be too old for a dinghy!"

Alec had discovered boats and the joy of rowing the first summer the Motts lived in the house overlooking Flounder Cove. The house had belonged to his grandfather, who now lived nearby in Rowbery. It was his grandfather who taught Alec to row. Ever since then Alec knew he *had* to have his own boat — to go out on the water and row and row whenever he needed to: as he had when he was new at the cove and the other boys ignored him; or now if he wanted to get

4

away from Jeannie; or if he just wanted to be in charge of what he was doing.

In the gathering crowd Alec also saw his friend, Scooty. Scooty had spent all his quarters playing the games and eating hot dogs and clam rolls. Scooty wouldn't be a competitor in the raffle because he didn't need the dinghy. He'd been sailing on his family's boat since he was big enough to fit into a life jacket, and, given a choice, Scooty preferred firm ground and a skateboard.

Then Alec saw his enemy, Stomper Gates. Actually he was Gilbert Gates, who lived two houses nearer Flounder Cove than Alec. Gilbert had acted early to make a name for himself other than his parents' loud "Bert-eee!" He stomped on ants, beetles, earwigs, and the tiny crabs trapped in the tide pools. Alec watched Stomper stroll over to the dinghy and put his hand on it and stroke it. He wondered how many tickets Stomper had. If Stomper won the boat, no one in the cove would be safe from his triumph and his scorn.

"Here we GO!" Mr. Keebler announced. "Now we'll open up this fine sea chest, and I am going to take this fine big wooden spoon Mrs. Pinkham had the foresight to bring, and we're going to stir, stir, stir these tickets all around. In fact, you take the spoon, Linda — ah, Miss Teen Annisconset — and I'll just plunge my hands right in here and mix and mix."

Alec was horrified. Linda was leaning over, holding her rhinestone tiara with one hand and stirring with the other. Like leaves on a swirling brook, Alec's tickets might have floated atop the eddies she made at one end of the chest. But Mr. Keebler, who ran the Annisconset Inn restaurant, was tossing tickets like salad greens — up and down, and up and down — with such vigor that some flew out of the chest and had to be poked back in, to the bottom. What if one of those was 1924, 1925, 1926, 1927, or 1928! A shudder shook Alec. Then he remembered what his mother always tried when she had to park the car in the city: Think Positive. It worked for her, too.

But he wasn't sure when to *start* thinking positive. The prize he wanted would be the last drawn. Thinking positive too soon could stick him with a crocheted blanket or a gallon of maple syrup. Maybe it should be done like: Ready, get set, and then an all-out GO at the last minute. So Alec started thinking: I can get a prize; I know I can; it will happen. How was that for positive!

Mr. Keebler's bleats into the mike drew the crowd over and at last the tickets were tossed enough to please him. "Pick a ticket!" he urged.

Miss Annisconset shut her eyes, worked her hand into the contents of the chest and pulled out the first plum. "Ooo-who has . . . number . . . eight-two?"

The fourth prizes were raffled off — the afghan, the syrup, the fruit basket, the year's supply of trash bags, the dinner for two at the Inn, and the Whale Watch tickets (for a moment, Alec regretted not having thought positive about those, but then, when he had the dinghy, he could do his own whale watching).

Then Mr. Keebler announced, "Now for the third prize — this handsome —"

"Excuse me," said Mrs. Pinkham. "That was only six fourth prizes. I thought we had one more."

"There's nothing more on this table, dear lady."

Mrs. Pinkham looked fussed. Alec remembered how she'd never lost track of so much as a Stalk of Celery or a Molar in their school plays. She knew there was a seventh fourth prize somewhere.

Mr. Keebler continued. Alec thought: I will get a prize. It will be THE prize. Dinghy, dinghy, dinghy.

"— authentic design sea chest with rope handles. Just like the ones sailors on clipper ships used to stow their belongings in on long voyages. Generously made and donated by Bill Pearce, our local woodworker. Linda, my dear, who's the lucky winner?"

"It says . . . six-four-eight!"

Alec's eyes were shut so tight, concentrating on the boat, he didn't know whether it was a tourist or a townsperson who won the chest.

"And now we come to this handsome oil painting by our well-known Annisconset summer resident and artist, who has generously donated a seascape this year. Thank you, Alice Butterick. Some family is going to be delighted to take this home."

As long as it isn't me, Alec thought. I wouldn't even take that picture for my mother (Alec was actually quite fond of his mother — most of the time). I want to be on the sea, in my boat, not looking at it in a frame on the wall.

7

"— four-three-three!" Linda announced, beating Mr. Keebler's mouth to the mike.

Alice Butterick's neighbor, old Miss Longley, sighed and waved her ticket. She had enough Buttericks — given in payment of rent on a small summer cottage — to start a gallery. But she gave a gallant Sea Fest smile, to encourage the tourists, and showed enthusiasm. There was no doubt Alice could paint rocks and boats and fishing shacks well. Still Alec wondered if Miss Longley thought the waves in the painting looked more like cake frosting than splashing seas. He did.

"And now the grand finale." Mr. Keebler had regained the mike. "This handsome dinghy, easily fitted up to be a sailing dinghy, if the winner so desires, has been donated by —"

Alec didn't listen to the credits. He was deep in concentration. His mind drilled the numbers over and over — 1924, 1925, 1926, 1927, 1928. He was sure he would win on the next draw. It was now a calm certainty in his heart, a sure knowledge in his head.

Then he heard Mrs. Pinkham's voice interrupting Mr. Keebler. He opened his eyes and his ears. She was rushing up to Mr. Keebler carrying a small bald baby. Alec was disgusted. Here he'd gotten all his energy together and put his positive thinking in motion, only to have the drawing interrupted. Of all the times for a mother to lose a baby!

But Mrs. Pinkham wasn't worried. She wasn't asking, "Who's lost a baby? Whose little boy is this?" She was laughing and saying, "I found him. I knew we

8

had him somewhere and sure enough — there he was, taking a nap in the dinghy. Linda, I see you have a number in your hand, but before we give away the dinghy, we should give away the last fourth prize. This little fellow is up for adoption. This is Christopher Elvis, everyone. Isn't he adorable?"

Giving away a baby! What had happened to Mrs. Pinkham and Annisconset! Alec was horrified. He was still blinking and clearing his eyes. They ached from being scrunched shut so hard while he thought positive.

Hold off! I don't want a fourth prize! Alec almost cried it out loud. Dinghy, dinghy, dinghy! he insisted in his head.

Miss Teen Annisconset looked at the number in her hand. "The winner of this wonderful Cabbage Patch doll — whose name is Christopher Elvis — is number one-nine-two-five."

2

"Number one-nine-two-five? Is number one-nine-two-five here?"

Alec kept the porch pillar between himself and Mr. Keebler. He wouldn't claim a Cabbage Patch doll. He'd never live it down. That number in Linda's hand when Mrs. Pinkham so fatefully interrupted had been drawn for the dinghy!

Suddenly Mr. Keebler's voice boomed over the PA system. "Now we've deciphered the name on this ticket stub and I can understand the reluctance of the holder of ticket one-nine-two-five to claim the prize. But he shouldn't be shy. He can be a thoughtful big brother and give a handsome present to his little sister. Come on, Alexander Mott — come claim this Cabbage Patch baby. He's all yours."

Alec heard yowls of laughter. And the loudest, meanest whoops came from Stomper Gates. Even Scooty was bursting with guffaws. Alec tried to retreat from the front of the porch but Mr. Keebler spotted him. "Come right over here and claim your prize, Alec."

"I don't want it," Alec said. "I wanted the dinghy. That ticket was drawn for the boat."

But no one heard him. Alec could tell that the crowd thought it was funny to see an eleven-year-old boy shocked by this solidly stuffed bald baby clad in diaper and plastic pants, its arms outlifted wistfully. It was equipped with a bag containing not only adoption papers but the works, and Miss Teen Annisconset insisted on listing them — bottle, pacifier, powder, more diapers.

Alec was totally mortified. What if Stomper Gates saw him with that doll in his hands? Stomper wouldn't have to stomp on Alec to grind his feelings. All he would ever have to do would be to mutter "Cabbage Patch Kid!" and even if Alec had become a hero, a great Olympic rower, Stomper would bring back this flush of embarrassment.

"Alec!" His father stood by the porch rail, with Jeannie still on his shoulders. "Give Jeannie the ticket. Let her collect the doll."

Alec looked at his father. He suspected one more case of his father favoring his little sister. But Mr. Mott gave him a truly sympathetic look. "Mr. Keebler's idea is good. Give Jeannie the ticket and you won't have to touch the stupid doll."

"Okay. But it would have been my boat, you know. That drawing was supposed to be for first prize. It's not fair."

"It doesn't seem fair. But it's what happened."

Stomper Gates was jigging up and down, yelling, "Alec has a baby!" Alec pushed all his stubs into

Jeannie's hand and fled to the side of the porch. He climbed over the railing and disappeared between the Town Hall and its bordering hedge. He didn't want to know who won the dinghy. The way things were going, it would probably be Stomper.

Alec didn't understand why his father always told him to play fair — "Don't cheat!" — and then shrugged this off as something that just happened. His father would probably say to his mother, "That was a rotten shame Alec came so close and then missed. But that's life."

So much for thinking positive.

The street behind the Town Hall was empty except for the parked cars that would soon be carrying the Sea Fest crowd home. Alec hurried away. He felt as if his T-shirt read ALEXANDER MOTT — WINNER OF CABBAGE PATCH BABY instead of ROW FOR IT.

❋

When Alec had discovered the shirt at the Sports Shop in Rowbery he'd bought it right away. He was sure it was a good omen. This year he was going to win the Rowbery Junior Rowers race.

Rowbery was a commercial fishing port. Whether the *Row* in the city's name had been the inspiration for it or not, the city sponsored a Race Week at the end of the summer. No sails. No motors. Just rowboats — from the heavy dories like those used by fishermen on the Grand Banks in the fishing-schooner days to the plastic tubs now used by kids in the baby races. Alec's grandfather, Old Lob Fittler, lived in

Rowbery. During Alec's first summer at Flounder Cove, when he was having trouble fitting in and wanting so much to prove himself, Old Lob had sponsored him in the Pee Wee race. He hadn't had much serious competition and he'd won the race. This year, in the Junior Rowers group of ten-, eleven-, and twelve-year-olds, it would be much harder to win.

And he didn't have a boat. His old pram had been smashed in a storm last autumn. His grandfather had promised to replace it.

At first his grandfather promised to build it himself. "Here I've been mucking about in boats all my life," Old Lob told him, "but I've never made one. Now I'm retired I can design a boat for you that will win every race. You name it and you got it."

"Let's name it after you."

"You want to call it the *Jasper Fittler?*"

"No. I mean after *you*. The *Old Lob*."

"Old Lobster Fittler. That's what people call me. The Old Lob who spent the best years of his life out on the water hauling pots. You know I held the record for the most pounds of lobsters sold by one man to the co-op in one year? Those were the days. Barely any lobsters left around here now."

"How do you build a boat?" Alec wanted his grandfather to stick to the point.

"A good question. And we've got a winter to do it in."

So Old Lob bought some books and some tools and he read about building boats. Whenever Alec took the

13

bus to Rowbery on a Saturday, he found books and drawings of boats all over the tables in the small apartment. Then he noticed the books were growing gray jackets of dust and the papers were yellowing. Alec's grandmother, a tidy duster-and-picker-upper, had died six years ago.

"When are you going to start building the *Old Lob?*" Alec had asked.

"You heard about the man who built a boat in his basement and then couldn't get it out the bulkhead door? Well, I don't even have a corner of this basement all to myself to work in. And they got a measly little door marked Exit. Can't barely get a couch through it. But —"

"How big a boat are you going to build?" Alec interrupted. Old Lob talked big. Think Positive was his mother's motto, but her father's motto was Think Big. Alec wondered if the boat would be too big for him to row!

"— and you got to have a steambox to bend wood. Now just last week I talked to Charlie Culp, the janitor, and he'd like to help us out, Alec. But he says the insurance company wouldn't allow a steambox in the basement. So you see — building a boat may not be as practical as you and I thought. We've got to think of some other way to get you a boat."

Alec had felt like a burst balloon tied to a string — a string that his grandfather was still holding. Once Old Lob got on to a project, he didn't stop talking about it. He'd keep saying he was going to do it, even if he never got around to it. But he'd be surprised and

14

hurt if anyone else took over and did it. Like the time he was going to make Alec's mother a rope hammock. After two hot summers went by, while Old Lob talked about the techniques of hammock weaving, she went out and bought one.

When they had to abandon the boat-building idea, Alec began haunting the boat yards, the coves, and the marshes. Dinghies in good condition at the boat yards cost more than he could ever save, and his hope of finding a boat washed up and abandoned, one he and his grandfather could fix up, hadn't happened. Winning the raffle had seemed like the perfect solution.

*

Although he had walked a short distance from the Town Hall, he suddenly heard applause and cheering. Someone had won his dinghy. Alec kicked a tire on a parked car. He wasn't going to have a lucky summer after all. Even if by some miracle an unsinkable boat came to him, he would barely have time enough to learn to handle it.

Alec knew boats were like people. Some were easy to get along with and some were not. He'd learned a lot hanging around boat yards and coves where fishermen and sailors moored their boats, listening to the talk. The boat owners either loved every inch of their crafts' planking—or, nowadays, fiberglass—or cursed their uncooperative ways. But he knew when he found his boat, when he learned how his boat felt about things, they would be an unbeatable pair.

15

3

"Why do they call a boat *she* instead of *it?*" Alec asked the next day at breakfast.

Even the new member of the family, Christopher Elvis, sat by the table in the old high chair. Alec hated seeing him there, with his stubby arms and hands spread out to invite hugs. He hated watching Jeannie tie a bib around his neck. He hated the smirky way she said, "Christopher Elvis loves you, Alec. He's so happy you let me adopt him."

"I didn't have anything to do with him. The Fickle Finger of Fate gave him to you, Creep-o, when it messed up on the dinghy. Mum, why are boats called —"

"I'm glad that you see your not winning the boat as a matter of fate or chance," Alec's father broke in, sounding like the lawyer he was. "It was just chance that Mrs. Pinkham saw that leftover fourth prize when she did. It was just chance that Linda was picking a ticket with your number on it when Mr. Keebler saw that another fourth prize should be given out before

16

the first prize. Last night you thought it wasn't fair —"

"It isn't!" Alec said. Last night he had felt angry and frustrated. This morning he felt hurt and let down.

Mr. Mott raised his hand, like a judge silencing a courtroom. (If things went well, Alec's father hoped to be a judge in another ten years.) "Fair, Alec, has to do with facts and the weighing of justice. Entering a raffle puts everything into the realm of chance — and chance has nothing to do with fairness. It's a random thing. Now, it's a rotten shame that you came so close to winning and then lost out. But it happened by chance, not by logic and rules."

"But —" Alec began.

"Look, guys," said Alec's mother. "I made blueberry pancakes to cheer you up. So enjoy them. Don't hold a seminar on fate and fairness. Alec is disappointed enough, Dan, without a lecture on raffles."

"You're right, Liz. My apologies, Alec. I know having your own boat seems very important to you."

"It is *very* important. And you didn't answer my question. Why is a boat called she? Like that sport-fishing boat that moored at the cove last week called *Old-Man-of-the-Sea* even though the man who owns it says 'she handles like a racing car.'"

"I wish *she* didn't," Mr. Mott said. "I watched that boat speed into the cove so fast she almost overran the mooring. I was afraid the boat would shoot right over the dock and up onto the road and wipe out the kids and the artists painting on the jetty."

"That man doesn't know any better, I guess," said

17

Alec. "I heard him tell Salty that he's never had a boat before."

"That's no excuse," said Mr. Mott. "In fact, it's all the more reason for him to learn powerboat rules and rules of the sea and to use them."

"Isn't there a warning sign on the sea wall about slowing down when you come in through the gap?" asked Mrs. Mott. "There used to be."

"The big storm last February ripped it off," said Alec.

"Whoever's in charge of the cove ought to put it back," said Mrs. Mott. Alec knew she had strong feelings about Flounder Cove.

Alec sometimes wondered why his mother and father had married each other when the way they grew up and what they talked about seemed so different. His father had been born and raised in Indiana. He didn't know anything about the seacoast and the ocean. He said he hadn't even thought much about the ocean until he met Alec's mother in college and she tried to tell him why she missed it so.

Alec had grown up hearing his mother's stories about the ocean and this very house the Motts lived in at Flounder Cove. The house had belonged to his grand-father before he moved to Rowbery. From the moment the Motts had moved in, Alec had shared his mother's interest in the activities around the cove, and he was delighted by her information about lobsters, fish, the tides, and the marine life between the tide lines. Flounder Cove was a wonderful place and Alec was glad that when his grandfather no longer wanted such a big house, his father had agreed to his mother's plea that they take the house and that he start a law practice in Rowbery.

Alec knew his mother really understood how he yearned for a good boat and she knew how deep his disappointment was when he won that creature who beamed from the high chair. Christopher Elvis Mott, indeed!

"Don't forget to pick up Dad and bring him over for supper," she reminded Mr. Mott, as he left to drive to his office.

The phone rang. Alec answered it, hoping it was Scooty and he'd be willing to go on an abandoned-boat search again. Instead, it was Miss Longley asking "Do you have time to help me in the yard this morning, Alec?" Occasionally she hired him to do things his mother expected him to do for free. He was delighted. He needed to earn money. Even if he found a boat that could float, he'd have to buy caulking and paint and oars. "I'll be right over," he promised.

Alec liked going to Miss Longley's house. He liked the way it stood out on the highest hill in Annisconset, looking like a big square wedding cake with a fancy frosting railing around a little square at the top. Miss Longley let Alec go up there sometimes and climb up into the walkway. "People used to call them widow's walks," she explained. "Several of my great-great-grandmothers were sea captains' widows. I've been told that one of them used to come up here and watch for her husband's clipper ship long after he and his ship went down in the China Seas. She turned a bit dotty about waiting for him."

The China Seas! Alec liked the adventurous sound of the words. He hoped to sail those seas himself someday.

In her front parlor Miss Longley had a curio cabinet. One rainy afternoon she had let Alec take things out of it while she told him about the pieces of scrimshaw — ivory whale bone with drawings etched and inked onto them by sailors. Intricate lanyards knotted in string. Enormous shells. Jade monkeys. Paper fans painted with scenes and Chinese characters.

Miss Longley met him by her front gate. "I hope you're in the mood to weed. I don't mind dandelions on my lawn in spring. I eat the leaves in salad. But I object to dandelions, buttercups, and cow parsley running loose in the flower beds. Let me show you the culprits. You can yank them out and fling them into that wheelbarrow, and we'll bag them for the trash collector. I won't let them near my compost pile."

Alec looked at the long strip of garden climbing toward the house on each side of the brick walk. It would take hours to weed to the front door and back. So much for his abandoned-boat-hunt plans.

She handed him her basket, in which she kept hand-weeders and trowels, gave him a brisk pat on the shoulder, and opened the gate. "I've heard a dreadful rumor, and I've got to find out if it's true. I'll be back soon." Alec wondered what was so dreadful that Miss

Longley would set off at such a fast pace.

Alec ripped into the weeds. Pulling up cow parsley was hard work. It grew a great web of roots and he pulled up too many flowers along with it. He felt relieved Miss Longley wasn't watching as he tamped the seedlings back in place.

What could the dreadful rumor be? There were always rumors around Flounder Cove. It looked like a peaceful place for men and boats. But there were problems. Lobstermen tried to keep scuba divers away so they wouldn't swim out and steal lobsters from their pots. Scuba divers complained that the lobstermen didn't own the rocks and the sea wall and the water in the cove or the ocean. Summer people who moored powerboats and sailboats there complained about fishermen leaving their stinking nets spread on the jetty to dry. The fishermen complained about people in sailboats drifting into their trap nets, and lobstermen complained about people in speedboats cutting pot lines with their propellers.

But Miss Longley would hardly be concerned with life at the cove. This had something to do with the other part of Annisconset life — that of the people in the big houses. Some of them lived there year-round and some only came during the summers.

He had yanked out weeds halfway along the first strip of garden when Miss Longley returned. She looked disgusted.

"Do you know a Mrs. Trowbridge?" she asked. "Although I don't know why you should. She's a newcomer. From some western state that runs to desert and mountains. She bought that handsome old house next to the Inn."

"What about her?"

"She won the dinghy."

"My dinghy? The prize my ticket was drawn for until Mrs. Pinkham saw that dumb doll?"

Alec thunked a large clump of cow parsley into the wheelbarrow. He wished he could thunk Mrs. Trowbridge too.

"Shockingly unfair," said Miss Longley, and Alec instantly pledged her his lifelong devotion. Although as she went on, he realized she was speaking of a different kind of unfairness. "For a woman with no sensitivity to the sea and its traditions to win a handsome rowboat designed and built by a master boat builder like Ezra Elliott is not right. What she is doing to it is a crime. It's unfair to Ezra's craft and to everyone who loves boats!"

"What! What is she doing to it?"

"She's putting it on her front lawn, filling it with dirt, and she's planting petunias in it."

4

"We've got to stop her!" Alec wanted to run to the rescue and start bailing dirt out of the boat.

"I agree," said Miss Longley, "but we need a plan. There's no law that says a person can't plant petunias in a rowboat on her own front lawn."

"Do you think if I explained to her that my number should have won it, she'd swap?"

"For that rather odd doll?"

"Maybe she likes odd things if she likes flowers in rowboats. But that wouldn't work even if she *would* swap. Jeannie thinks Christopher Elvis is hers. She's already adopted him." Alec shuddered. He was talking as if Christopher Elvis were alive. His world was topsy-turvy. Boats were planted; toys were considered human. An earthquake couldn't have shaken him more.

"Aha!" Miss Longley exclaimed. "Maybe she'd swap it for that painting I won. I'll even throw in another of Alice Butterick's paintings, if it would make a deal. Let's take them over right now. Perhaps we can persuade Mrs. Trowbridge to become an art collector."

A large framed painting was an awkward object, Alec discovered. If he carried it like a suitcase, it bumped now and then on the ground. He tried holding it out in front of him like a tray. He tried one grip after another. His arms ached by the time they turned into the road by the river channel — a street lined with graceful trees, trim lawns and gardens, and large white houses with a view of the marshes and tidal creeks on the far side of the river.

Alec saw a yellow pickup truck filled with loam. Beyond it, resting on a crest of the lawn, was the dinghy. Nearby, flats of petunias made ruffled rows of white, pink, and purple. And standing by the flowers, telling a man in work clothes what to do, was Mrs. Trowbridge. She was a large woman dressed in blue jeans, a Western-style shirt, and a high-crowned, broad-brimmed straw hat. Her cowboy boots had shaped heels that would have knocked a hole in a more fragile boat than the dinghy.

Alec and Miss Longley rested the paintings against a tree trunk and listened up, almost as if Mrs. Trowbridge had ordered them to. Alec had to listen extra hard because he'd never heard anyone talk the way she did — slowly and with each word having more sounds in it than he expected.

Mrs. Trowbridge was telling Grover Tarr what she wanted and how to do it. When she saw Alec and Miss Longley, she gave them a friendly smile and then asked their advice. "You-all been observing. Do you think that little bitty boat is going to show up enough there on that lawn? To show a name and address? I mean, we'll paint *Trowbridge 9 River Channel Road* on the side so people will know it's us. Down home we have a big arch over the driveway. It says *Happy Haven Ranch* and we shine a spotlight on it at night. You can read the name a quarter mile away."

At least that's what Alec thought she said when he'd straightened out her stretched-out way of talking.

"I think," said Miss Longley, "people will find your address without your having to — well, to worry about using the boat as a sign. As a matter of fact, before Mr. Tarr shovels any more dirt into the dinghy, Alec Mott would like to talk to you about it."

"Yes, boy?" Mrs. Trowbridge had picked up an oar and she poked the curve of the blade into the lawn and leaned on it. Alec winced.

"It's just that — well, I really should have won the boat in that raffle. Linda — Miss Teen Annisconset — already had drawn the ticket that was supposed to be the last ticket. For the first prize. The dinghy. Then Mrs. Pinkham saw that Cabbage Patch Kid lying in the boat and she and Mr. Keebler decided it had to be given as a prize before the boat was. And I got it instead of the dinghy. You wouldn't want to swap, would you? By rights, you would have won Christopher Elvis."

"I know there was a huffin' puffin' furor over those doll kids last year. But I hardly think it would be a good horse trade — like we do down home — to swap a doll I can't use for a boat that is going to look like it's riding on a nice green sea with a pretty crew of flowers in it. What Mr. Trowbridge and I admire about New

25

England is it's so picturesque. Down on Cape Cod when I saw a boat full of flowers, I knew right away it would be the most picturesque way to show where Nine River Channel Road is. And how about these paddles! I certainly want to use them. Maybe in an arch over the drive?"

Alec looked at the oar she was leaning on. His gaze followed its clean line, the beautiful proportion of its blade to its handle. He could almost feel the strength of the tight-grained wood in his grasp, as he mentally curved his fingers around a pair of oars. He knew how deftly he could dip the blades into the water so that they pulled the boat ahead. Then he would feather the oars, or turn them, so that they slid up again, dripping but not splashing. And that dinghy! He stepped toward it and looked at the carefully crafted wood — the subtle curve of the bottom, the sides shaped for steadiness and also to slip easily through the water after the peaked bow, the wooden seats placed to balance the passengers' weight. It was a sweet boat. A boat he could row to win.

Mr. Tarr threw a shovelful of loam that splatted onto the boat's bottom. Alec turned away. Every thud of dirt was a blow to him. It was an insult to the man who crafted the dinghy.

"Hold on now!" said Miss Longley. "I respect your horse-trading tradition, Mrs. Trowbridge. It's an old New England tradition, too. And I think you and I could make a more reasonable trade than Alec can offer you."

Another spadeful of dirt thudded into the boat. Mr. Tarr didn't believe in standing idle when he was being paid to work.

Mrs. Trowbridge stepped closer to Miss Longley. "What have you got in mind?"

"I know that boat is worth a good bit of money. Ezra Elliott is famous for his dinghies."

Alec tried not to groan. Why was Miss Longley telling Mrs. Trowbridge the boat was valuable? She'd want all the more to keep it.

"Also his boats are much too seaworthy to spend their days holding up petunias. Now I am prepared to swap you two of Alice Butterick's paintings. They are very New England, very picturesque, let me assure you."

Alec laid the paintings on the lawn by Mrs. Trowbridge's boots. She did not seem impressed.

"The color's nice. But those frames are skimpy. Back home we have some paintings of Mr. Trowbridge's prize steers and they're fitted out with gorgeous gold frames with curlicues."

"I'm sure Alice Butterick's seascapes would look handsome in bigger frames and the Framery in Rowbery is very good."

"Well, I don't know. I had my heart set on prettyin' up the front yard and doin' somethin' special. Just puttin' up pictures inside the house doesn't do much for the neighborhood."

"It would do a lot for Alice Butterick," suggested Miss Longley. "You'd be a real art patron. And, speak-

27

ing of being neighborly, if you will swap the boat for the paintings, I will gladly put your name up as a member of the Garden Club."

Alec thought he knew what Miss Longley wasn't saying: "We'll put you in the Garden Club and keep an eye on what you do in your yard!" But Mrs. Trowbridge heard the invitation, not the threat.

"Done!" she said. "Grover, just shovel that dirt back out of that boat and we'll figure out what to do with it. Boy, you take those pictures up and put them on the front porch."

When Alec came back, Mrs. Trowbridge tipped him a dollar and Miss Longley winked at him. "Alec, will you take those oars along and store them in my back entry? Then finish the weeding. I'm going to help Mrs. Trowbridge plan a rock garden just about where the boat is now, and Mr. Tarr will move the boat in his truck later on."

Alec shouldered the oars. As he hiked along the street, he wondered, what Miss Longley would do with the boat. Did she really want to keep it? Or did she just want to stop Mrs. Trowbridge from ruining the planking and upsetting the neighborhood? Would she make him a swap for it? And if she would, what could he give her? .

5

Alec looked up when he heard the muttering approach of Grover Tarr's truck. Miss Longley leaned out of the cab's window. "Alec — bring the oars and come to the cove with us."

At least Miss Longley planned to put the boat in the water! Since she felt so strongly about rescuing it, maybe she even knew how to row. Maybe she'd let Alec go out with her and he could say, "Miss Longley, when you get tired, I'll be glad to row for a while."

Alec slipped the oars into the back of the pickup. He wanted to ride to the cove sitting in the dinghy. It would be like riding on a float in a parade. But Miss Longley ordered him into the cab beside her.

"I'm putting the boat in the cove," she said. "Years ago we kept our boats there. My two brothers and I each had our own and it was exciting to row out early in the morning and fish for flounder. My brothers used to drift around and try different spots. I used to anchor and be patient. I usually caught more fish than they did."

"You baited your own hook? And took the fish off

the hook yourself?" Grover Tarr asked. "How did I miss you! That used to be my test for whether I took a girl out fishing more than once."

"I used to bait, unhook, and clean my fish. My father taught me how," Miss Longley announced. "And my mother taught my brothers to make bread. My parents believed in what they called 'the well-rounded child.' "

That was an expression Alec had never heard before. Looking at tall and trim Miss Longley now, he had trouble thinking of her as well-rounded in any way.

Grover swung the truck downhill into the cove road. They drove past Alec's house. He hoped Jeannie and Christopher Elvis were on the porch and would see him looking important in Grover Tarr's truck. Maybe they would even think he'd somehow become the owner of the dinghy.

"Where are you going to moor her?" Alec asked. Grover stopped on the stone-topped jetty in the middle of the cove.

Miss Longley looked with dismay over the edge of the jetty at the crowd of small boats tied to rungs of ladders or swinging about on rope-and-buoy rigs that could pull them to shore. "What a lot of boats! I was daydreaming to think that the ladders we used years ago would still be here and be free."

Alec agreed. The cove was overcrowded. The rocking wake of a motorboat would send any number of hulls grinding into each other.

Grover Tarr cleared his throat. "Mind if I unload your dinghy on the jetty? I'm supposed to be moving dirt back at the Trowbridge place."

"Of course you are! Alec — give Mr. Tarr a hand, please."

It was heavy work, helping Grover pull out the dinghy and put it down. Even as Alec grunted with the unexpected weight, he was delighted by it. This dinghy was no peanut shell to be tossed about by the slap of a wave or a push of the wind. This was a boat that would carve a groove in the water, that would build up momentum and glide on after each pull at the oars. Alec stood back and looked with love at her clean lines, her balance. He dreamed of gliding her over the finish line in Rowbery Harbor as thousands cheered.

"Alec!" Miss Longley's voice pulled him back to the jetty. "You will have to help me out here. First, I'll need a mooring. You know the cove and the men who use it. Is there anyone in charge?"

"Salty Ferris is always telling people what they can do. Or where not to do something. Like 'Don't leave that boat at the float overnight,' or 'Don't come speeding through the gap.' He's the first one here in the morning so if anyone's in charge, I guess he is."

"All right. You ask Salty Ferris where I can get a mooring — and if there's any expense, I'll pay for it. But I'm going to need someone to take care of the boat for me. To see it's riding right and won't be bumped about. And to bail it out after it rains."

"And see the oars don't go missing!" suggested Alec. He knew how kids fooled around in people's dinghies because he'd done it himself.

"Will you take care of the boat for me?"

31

"Absolutely!" Alec was relieved. "Will you take it out often?"

Miss Longley looked surprised. "Go rowing? Go fishing? Do you know — I hadn't really thought beyond rescuing it from the Trowbridge lawn and putting it in the water where it belongs. Yes. I should like to go flounder fishing once in a while."

"Can you still row?"

"I expect so. It's probably like riding a bicycle. Once you've learned, a little practice brings it back. Or did you mean — quite kindly I'm sure — am I still *able* to row?"

Alec gulped.

Miss Longley laughed. "I am exceptionally fit for my years. But if I go fishing, I'd be glad of your company. Rowing out is always easier than rowing back."

"I know. That's the hardest part of training."

"Training? Do you take rowing seriously?"

"I won the Pee Wee Class trophy at Rowbery Race Week, when I was eight. Now I'm in the Junior Rowers Class, but I don't have a boat. My grandfather was going to build me one. But it didn't work out."

"And that's why you were so disappointed when you didn't win the raffle?"

"Yes."

"I suppose a boat in the cove is like a horse in a stable. Exercise would be the best thing for it. You wouldn't like to use my boat to train in, would you?"

"And borrow it for Race Week?"

"And borrow it for Race Week."

"Oh! Thanks, Miss Longley! She's the most beautiful boat for racing."

"Well, you get her into the water and see what you can do. But I expect you tomorrow morning to finish off my weeds."

Miss Longley walked away and left Alec to handle the boat business by himself. He put the oars in the dinghy and ran along the jetty to the shack where Salty was pretending to be busy at something besides watching what was going on around the cove.

Salty didn't waste words and he sounded gruff when he yelled at kids or inept boatmen. But Alec had discovered something. Salty told wonderful stories and once when Alec had sat and listened to some and then brought Scooty to listen, too, the old man had pronounced them good kids. "Not troublemakers like some around here I could name but I won't." He also knew how badly Alec wanted a boat.

"What you done, Alec? Some mighty smart talkin'? I heard that boat was goin' to be sproutin' petunias by noontime."

"It was. But Miss Longley saved it. It's hers now. She asked me to get a mooring for it. Where can I put it?"

"Well, that's a problem. I don't know as there's one spot left free. Seems like the cove's more popular than it ever was, even with the breach in the sea wall."

"There's got to be a place. If Miss Longley has to moor this at the Yacht Club, I'll never get to use it."

"You're going to use it, eh?"

"For Rowbery Race Week. And for training."

"In that case, we'll have to make room. Tell you what — if you don't mind scrambling over the rocks that got knocked over on the breakwater, there's a mooring no one's using because it's hard to get to the ladder. I can help you rig up a buoy and a pulley so's you can run the boat in to the ladder. You look over in that corner and see if you can find some rope."

Alec knew that looking into corners in Salty's shack was like exploring a cave filled with rubbish. Poking about made him think of little Jack Horner sitting in a corner and putting in his thumb and pulling out a plum. But he felt more like a little Jack *Horror* as he pulled out a bag of dried sea worms and a rusty bait knife. Then he found a coil of rope. As Salty helped him haul it out, they dislodged a clanking of old buckets and tins of nuts and bolts caught in scraps of faded netting, which Salty kicked back toward the corner. Alec thought it would be great to be Salty and be able to keep his room junky, or clean it by kicking things aside.

"What you goin' to name her?" Salty asked, as he admired the dinghy's trim lines.

"She's not my boat and Miss Longley didn't say."

"Just askin'. Because it's a lot easier to paint a name while she's firm on the jetty than tiltin' in the water."

Alec looked at the road curving uphill from the cove. Miss Longley had stopped to sit on a wall and enjoy the view over the bay. When Alec caught up to her, she seemed to be daydreaming and he spoke quietly. He didn't want to startle her.

34

"I've got a mooring. Salty's giving us rope and will help rig the buoy and the pulley. But we need something else."

Miss Longley turned from gazing at the stretch of the bay and the low line of hills on its faraway shore. "Alec! You caught me being nostalgic. Pretending I wasn't a minute older than twelve and my brothers would come rowing through the gap. Now — what do we need?"

"A name for your boat. Salty says we should paint it before we put it in the water."

"A name!" Miss Longley looked pleased. "There are such lovely names for boats." She murmured names with lilting sounds. "Cythera. Isolde. Aphrodite. But those are better for sailboats — sort of slipping-through-the-water names. Running-before-the-wind names."

"How about names I can spell!" Alec exclaimed.

"You are a practical young man. Would you like a short name, too, so it won't take too long to paint?"

"Too right!" Alec agreed.

"When my brothers and I had our boats, they were named *Wynken, Blynken,* and *Nod.* Mine was *Nod.* That's short."

"*Nod?* and *Wynken* and *Blynken?*"

"From a poem our mother used to say at bedtime —

'*Wynken, Blynken, and Nod one night*
Sailed off in a wooden shoe —
Sailed on a river of crystal light
Into a sea of dew.'"

35

Alec hoped she wouldn't want to name her boat *Nod* or *Nod II*. Her dinghy was no wooden shoe. And as for sailing into a sea of dew — what a strange poem!

But Miss Longley went on. "I don't like short names. They sound so final. Like Maud. Or Jane. People try to soften them up and say Maudie or Janie. I don't think when you're my age that being a Maud*ie* or a Jan*ie* is fitting."

"What is your name?" Alec had never thought of her as anything but *OldMissLongley*.

"Helena. And I never had 'the face that launched a thousand ships' that you hear about in Greek myths. So it is not an appropriate choice. What do you suggest?"

"I've thought of one. But you might not like it."

"A woman's name?"

"Yes."

"Short?"

"Yes."

"Do you like it?"

"Yes."

"Then it meets the needs. Go ahead and paint it. I do like surprises."

Alec walked with her as far as his house. In the garage he found a can of green paint and a small paint brush. Three hours later one more boat floated in the cove, a trim dinghy whose white hull reflected in bright zigzags in the water and whose name was painted in green letters that wobbled only slightly.

She was the *Miss L.*

6

"Can I use Dad's stopwatch?" Alec asked his mother. He knew his father kept one in the leather box on his bureau, along with his tie clasps and cuff links and the medals he'd won for track events when he was in college.

"You'll have to ask him. His track coach — a man he thought the world of — gave it to him. Your father was a fine runner, you know."

Alec knew. His father often talked about how wonderful it was to run. How when you won a race even the exhaustion and the pain were worth it. "You have to get in there and give it all you've got," he was fond of telling Alec. "Competition. That's what makes the world go round."

Alec couldn't understand, if his father was so keen on competition, why he was uneasy about competing when it came to Alec's doing it in a boat. Maybe racing sailboats was scary and dangerous at times — but rowboats? Inside the harbor? It didn't make sense. How he wished his father had been a sailor, a man moved by the ocean and the winds — not one who found his highs on solid ground by putting down one foot after the other as fast as he could.

As Alec thought more about it, he realized his father never put on trunks and ran down to the cove to jump in the water and cool off on a hot night. When they went on family picnics to the long beach beyond Rowbery, his father spent his time running on the hard sand at the water's edge. The only time Alec's father ever got wet was in the shower.

That thought stunned Alec. He didn't even wince when Jeannie, who was spooning Flaky Fun cereal at Christopher Elvis, said, "Eat your cereal, Alec, so Christopher Elvis will eat his. You have to be a good uncle and set a good example."

"Mum, does Dad know how to swim? He doesn't ever go swimming!"

"He swam in a quarry when he was a boy. He's talked about how deep it was. He just doesn't like salt water. It makes him itch."

"He could take a shower afterward."

"So he could. But he says he likes running better than swimming."

"You and Dad sure are different! I mean, you love swimming and boats and fishing and mucking around at low tide. And the cove. I asked Dad if he wanted to go out in the *Miss L.* and he said he'd leave the rowing to you and me."

"We are different. But don't knock your father for not liking to swim and muck about in boats. He didn't grow up with them the way I did. And because he knew how homesick I was all the time in Indiana, when Dad wanted us to take over this house, he said, 'Let's do it.' He's the one who took a chance and started a new practice in Rowbery. You and I should always remember that." She brushed some crumbs off the table into her hand. "How's your love affair with the *Miss L.* coming along?"

"We're getting used to each other. I'm not catching crabs as much as I did."

"I hate it when you leave crabs in a pail on the porch and they stink," said Jeannie. "Wipe your chin, Christopher Elvis. That's a good boy."

"I'm not catching those kinds of crabs, Creep-o. Catching a crab when you're rowing is not catching the water right with your oar and making a splash."

"That doesn't make sense," said Jeannie. "How can you catch water?"

"It's easy if you do it right. It's called rowing." Alec left the table. He left the room. He liked to leave Jeannie with her mouth open, thinking of what to say back.

He ran upstairs to get his sweat shirt and as he passed his parents' room, he looked in and saw the leather box on the bureau. His father wouldn't be home until supper time. Alec wanted the stopwatch now. He reviewed the conversation with his mother. She hadn't actually said he couldn't take it. She'd said, "Ask your father." Well, he would. He'd borrow the watch now and put it back in the box and then ask his father at supper.

Alec opened the box. The watch was the biggest thing in it. He took it out and pushed the timer. The second hand began to click. He gave it ten seconds and pushed the timer again. The hand stopped. Ten seconds trapped onto the face of the watch. He released the second hand and it snapped back to zero.

He'd taken the watch out once before — the day he and Scooty timed how long they could hold their breath. Alec had been bragging about beating Scooty. One hundred and ten seconds to ninety-five! Then his father had walked in and found them playing with the watch.

"Please put it back," he'd told Alec. "It's not a toy."

Alec remembered that his father hadn't scolded him. He'd just said, "One hundred and ten seconds can seem like forever. Or it can't be long enough." And when Alec had asked, "What do you mean?" he'd walked out without explaining. Perhaps it had to do with a race he'd lost.

Alec closed the box and slid the stopwatch into a pocket in his shorts.

Outdoors his mother was trying to be patient with Jeannie, who insisted on putting the old baby seat into the car for Christopher Elvis before they went grocery shopping. He told her he was off for a training session and fetched the oars from the back porch.

At the cove he looked around for Scooty. He could take him along as coach and timekeeper. Scooty could call out the time for each leg of the course and then Alec wouldn't have to break off his stroke to look at the watch.

When he didn't see Scooty, he noticed that the *Windward HoHo IV*, the Merrill family's boat, wasn't in the cove and there was a brisk wind. A good day for sailing. He guessed that Scooty had been shanghaied for crew. Alec was picking his way over the rubble where the breakwater wall had fallen down, when he heard a splash. He looked up to see the *Miss L.* rocking violently. Someone had been hanging onto her and had pushed hard against her in swimming away. Under water. Alec stood still and watched the surface of the cove. He didn't see a head popping up, but soon he heard boys laughing. The sound came from behind a lobster boat moored beyond the *Miss L.*

It was midtide, and Alec could jump down into the boat after he'd descended six rungs on the ladder. He didn't though, because when he leaned over to drop in the oars, he saw what had been emptied into the boat. It was a mess of overripe fish heads and guts along with dead crabs and bent beer cans.

"Pee-yew!" Alec exclaimed. Another burst of laughter rose up from behind the lobster boat. Alec was sure he recognized a distinctively nasty chuckle. "Okay, Stomper. You stink worse than the fish guts."

As Alec bailed out the stuff with a bucket and then sluiced down the seats and the bottom and sponged it all clean, he was glad Miss Longley had changed her mind about taking a trip out on the bay with him that afternoon. If she'd seen what Stomper had done to the boat, she might have moved it over to the Yacht Club and let some other kid take care of it.

He unhooked the lines securing the dinghy and paddled with one oar through the cluster of hulls swinging at their moorings. He passed trim Star boats, old wooden lobster boats, sleek fiberglass sport-fishing boats, speedboats, and the battered hulk that belonged to the man who called himself Pirate Pete of Flounder Cove. Pirate Pete was bald, and he wore a beard and one gold earring. He dove for sea urchins, which went to Italian markets and fancy restaurants. Pete was getting ready to go out as Alec settled both oars into the oarlocks. "Someone trash your boat?"

"Yeah. And it's not my boat. So they better not do it again. She belongs to Miss Longley."

"Then you better make that a loud public announcement. But maybe it won't happen again. It's kind of a stupid standard initiation for a newcomer in the cove."

"I'm not a newcomer. I've been here four years now."

"Well, you weren't born here and your boat's new. Did Ezra Elliott build her? Looks like his lines."

"He did. She's the Sea Fest raffle boat. I'm training for the Junior Rowers race at Rowbery."

"So — maybe that explains the trash. You've got a rival."

Alec looked to where Pirate Pete was pointing and saw Stomper hoisting himself over the side of a dinghy wallowing at the mooring of the powerboat that belonged to the Gates family. The boat looked as new as the *Miss L.* In fact, she looked just like the *Miss L.* except that she had a red stripe painted around the hull for trim and at the stern the stripe zigzagged down like a lightning bolt. Lettered across in bold black was her name — *Flashdance.*

42

"Built by Ezra Elliott?" Alec asked Pete.

"Sure is. The Gateses had a blast of a launching and christening party down here last night. I'm surprised you didn't hear it."

"I was visiting my grandfather in Rowbery."

"Lucky you. I know your grandfather. Lob Fittler's a great guy. He's the one told me all the best spots for harvesting sea urchins."

Alec drifted as he watched Stomper pulling away from his mooring, heading for the gap in the breakwater. He decided to let Stomper shoot through first with his new boat and watch Stomper's style of rowing. So far he was splashing a lot of water. "They should have called her *Splashdance*," he said to Pete. "Stomper wanted to win the raffle as much as I did. He's lucky his dad could buy him a boat."

"You're pretty well matched, you two. He's maybe heavier and taller, but you'll have an edge on him if you keep working as hard as you have all week. You've got discipline I've never noticed in Stomper. So go on — get out there and good luck."

Alec squirmed more firmly onto the seat, braced his feet, and pulled. He'd oiled the oarlocks so they wouldn't screech with each stroke. He tried to forget about Stomper and *Flashdance* and to concentrate on long even pulls. The sea was choppy, with bursts of little rough wavelets that slapped and shoved the hull and made it hard to keep on the training course he'd worked out.

The course was shaped like a baseball diamond, only

much bigger. Just outside the gap in the breakwater was home plate; the orange float marking one end of Salty's trap net was first base; the bell buoy that kept up a metallic cling-clonk to the ocean's rhythms was second base; and third base was a point he had to fix for himself — where a straight line drawn out from the church steeple would cross a straight line drawn over from the lighthouse at the end of Annisconset Point. Alec was proud of that bit of navigation and quite sure he turned at the same invisible mark on the water each time. It was important, now that he could time himself, that the distance always be the same.

He put the stopwatch on the stern seat which was in front of him, since rowing a boat was something you usually did backwards. That is, you looked at where you'd been instead of where you were going. You had to sneak a peek over your shoulder to see if you were truly on course and aimed at your goal, though you could line up some object on shore and keep it in view as a heading while you tried to row a straight line out from it. Alec was getting better at that. The big problem outside Flounder Cove wasn't markers and goals — it was lobster pots and buoys, and not seeing them ahead until it was too late and your oar caught on a line. The only easy thing about the races in Rowbery Harbor was that there weren't any pots to tangle with.

Alec pushed the timer on the watch, and then leaned into the task. He would time himself over the whole course and set himself a time to beat. He tried to keep up a steady, even pull on the oars, but it was too choppy to get much of a glide between pulls, and he found he had to work harder with one oar to keep from being pushed off course.

Checking over his shoulder, he could see the large orange float that marked one corner of Salty's net. Alec swung the boat onto the second leg. He listened for the cling-clonk, cling-clonk of the bell buoy and tried to steer for it. The motor on a lobster boat started up with a prolonged coughing spell, and soon the boat's wake rocked the *Miss L.* roughly, up one side of its troughs and down the other, four tippy times. The noise of the boat drowned out the bell buoy and Alec looked over his shoulder just in time to turn away from running into it. With the buoy to sight on, the next leg of the course was easy, and Alec soon fixed his imaginary third base turning point and pulled for the breakwater. As he saw the gap at the edge of his vision on the left, he shipped the oars and pushed the timer. Twenty-four minutes and eighteen seconds. He knew his course wasn't as large as the one set out for the Junior Rowers. That usually took over half an hour for the best time. But this gave him something to work for. Maybe he could cut thirty seconds off his time each day.

Alec set off once more, but this time he was tired and he caught a lobster pot buoy with such a pull that the oar bounced out of his hand. He had to paddle after it. It took him almost twenty-nine minutes to complete the course. He rowed into the cove feeling as if he'd been trying to lift weights too heavy for him.

The *Miss L.* had changed from a bouncy skiff dancing over the waves to a barge lumbering along with a full cargo. Alec was so wet with sweat he felt as if he'd come up dripping from a dive.

Stomper hailed him from where he was securing *Flashdance* to the Gateses' mooring. "You got a slow scow there, Mott. *Flashdance* and I went to the lighthouse and back while you were just out to the bell buoy and back."

"Twice."

"Gimme a ride. I gotta leave the dinghy here for my folks when they bring the powerboat back."

Alec hesitated. It was an unwritten law of the cove that you ferried anyone who needed a lift, but he didn't want Stomper as a passenger. "Why don't you swim in?"

"Tide's too low. Water's too yucky."

"Does that bother you? I thought you didn't mind splashing around with fish guts."

He caught Stomper looking at *Miss L.*'s bottom. Probably wondering if Alec had cleaned up the mess. Then as Alec's boat slid by, Stomper grabbed the gunwale and jumped into *Miss L.* The stopwatch slid across the stern seat and Stomper grabbed it as he sat down.

"Give that to me," Alec said.

Stomper held it out of Alec's reach and played with the timer. "See how fast you can hit the breakwater. I'll give you — sixty seconds!"

Alec took the challenge — too hard and too fast. An

oar plopped up from the surface with a splash that caught Stomper, who glared at Alec.

"Forget timing me," said Alec as they edged between some boats. "Just give me the watch and catch the ladder."

"Sure." Stomper tossed the watch at him while Alec had both hands on the oars. He couldn't catch it in time. It hit the gunwale and spun off into the water.

Alec's heart spun with it as he saw it sink out of sight.

7

Alec wanted to whack Stomper over the head with an oar. "That's my father's prize stopwatch! He'll kill you!"

If only it could be Stomper that his father would tangle with. But he knew his father would place the blame on the boy who shouldn't have taken the watch to begin with. Alec himself. In his gut he had a cramp of fright.

Yet maybe the situation wasn't hopeless. If he could find the watch quickly, maybe the salt water wouldn't ruin it. Instead of whacking Stomper, Alec leaned out of the dinghy and poked at the bottom with the oar, hoping to catch sight of the bright metal case.

Stomper leapt for the ladder. "Tough you-know-what to you, Mott. Lucky you're *short*. You can just reach down and pick it up. Now I'd have to dive for it!"

Alec despaired. It was bad enough to be responsible for what his father would surely view as a crime. Alec heard in his head a fearful roll call of legal phrases from his father's vocabulary: unlawful possession, willful act, something that sounded like *hay-nus* crime (whatever that meant). There was no doubt about it. He had willfully taken unlawful possession of the stopwatch and to his father that would be a heinous crime indeed. But the ultimate blow was Stomper's calling him short. His below-average height caused Alec a lot of another of his father's phrases: mental anguish. And physical anguish, too. He'd been picked on more than once by the bigger boys who waited at the school bus stop. In fact, Alec often took an extra-long walk so he could use a different stop. He told himself it was because he liked Nancy Wentworth, who waited there, and he hoped that someday Nancy would say more than "Hi" to him.

Alec had not developed enough self-confidence to ignore the hurt of having his height scorned by Stomper, but he had developed some self-control along with quick wits. As far as possible he tried to think himself out of situations. So now was not the time to go after Stomper. He flung the bow line around a ladder rung in a quick hitch and slid into the water. He was glad he'd worn his deck sneakers to keep his feet from slipping and sliding in the boat as he braced his legs for heaving at the oars. The bottom of the cove had broken glass and rusted fish hooks stuck in the muck and he knew there were sharp barnacles and mussel shells on the slippery rocks. As his feet touched the bottom a few feet from the wall he kicked up some silt. The water was cold and it came up to his armpits.

Alec waited until the water cleared, took a deep breath, ducked under, opened his eyes, and looked around. His knees and his feet suddenly seemed huge. A fish that came wiggling past looked large enough for a meal, but he knew that out of water it would be only a snack — like a sardine. Banners of seaweed fanned out over his sneakers and then drifted together, pushed and pulled by the waves.

As Alec moved his feet, which felt as if they didn't quite belong to him down there, he saw a flash of metal and lunged for it. Once his fingers touched it, he let go. It was only the pull-ring of a beer can. Soon he felt the column of his breath being pinched out. He straightened up, thrusting his head into the air and gasping.

After another try, he realized he could see more of the bottom more quickly if he swam over it than if he walked, even though his sopping sneakers made his feet feel like weights. As he swam underwater, he could see the stones and the mud and the weeds and the old fish carcasses that rested on the bottom. And — at last — the watch! He picked it out from under some swaying fronds of seaweed just as he was running out of air again.

Alec stood in the cold water, shaking the watch, and holding it to his ear. Nothing! It had stopped. He felt as if his stomach and lungs and heart had stopped, too. The next time his father took the watch out of his leather box and pushed the timer and nothing happened, would he think the watch had died of old age? Then Alec laughed. Of course! Shaking wouldn't start this watch. He pushed the timer, and to his joy the hand began racing past the numbers. It worked!

He'd wipe it dry and tuck it into the box and his father would never know.

"Hi there!"

Alec looked up to see his mother at the top of the ladder. She was smiling at him, but he recognized it as what she called an "I'm smiling because I do love you but we need to talk" smile. There was no doubt she knew exactly what Alec had in his hand and exactly what had just happened to it.

"Hi, Mum."

"How's the water?"

"Cold."

"How did the training go?"

"Okay. The first time. The second was slow."

"Are you through for the day? Or would you like to show me what you can do?"

"I'm through. And, Mum —" He opened his hands so she could see the watch. "It got wet. Will the salt water ruin it?"

"Maybe not if you get it thoroughly dry. Do you think Miss Longley would mind if I took her dinghy for a quick row?"

"I guess not."

"You don't need her permission?"

"No. She trusts me to take good care of the boat. I wouldn't let anyone else but you use it."

"I'm glad she can trust you."

Alec knew his mother was underlining something without actually saying it to him.

"Mum — I took Dad's watch without asking him."

"I know. He happened to call up about something,

51

so I told him how anxious you were to start timing your workouts and you were going to ask if you could use the watch. He knows how important training and timing are for any kind of race. So he said you could. I was going to tell you when you came in. Then I looked in the box and the watch wasn't there. Look, Alec — come out of that cold water and snug down here in the sun while I row. Here's a towel. Keep the watch in the sun, too, and just figure out how you're going to tell Dad about how it took a bath."

Alec flung the towel over one of the flat stones at the end of the breakwater and stretched out. The sun placed a warm touch on his back. After seeing his mother skillfully work the *Miss L.* through the moored boats and out the gap, he closed his eyes and shut himself away from the dazzle of light flashing off the metal watch case. He knew there was only one way to tell his father anything: as any witness in court had to swear, he would have to tell the truth, the whole truth, and nothing but the truth to deserve his father's fair judgment about his situation. It wouldn't be easy. In spite of the warmth of the sun, he shivered.

His mother climbed the ladder after deftly clipping the *Miss L.* to her line and playing her out to the mooring. "She's a lovely little skiff. Perfect for racing. An Ezra Elliott boat should give you an edge on the competition."

"Did you see Stomper's boat? The *Flashdance?*"

"At their mooring? Oh, my! You've got twins!"

"So much for the edge." Alec shrugged.

"Oh? Doesn't it mean you both have an advantage

over any other kind of dinghy — and you'll each have
to take it from there?"

"I guess so."

"I thought you really wanted to win."

"I do, but —" Alec stopped. He did want to win. So
no buts. He grinned at his mother. "Lunch?"

"Lunch. Rowing is unfortunately as good for the
appetite as it is for the figure."

During the afternoon Alec went over to Miss Longley's and helped her with her vegetable garden. He
chopped away at weeds in her corn patch while she
patiently thinned the carrots. He did tell her about
Stomper's trashing her boat and how he'd cleaned it
up and his training course and Stomper's having a
twin to the *Miss L.*

She told him that she'd been up on her widow's
walk that morning with her telescope. "Just watching
the world going about its business. Fascinating. Do
you realize if there weren't any people anywhere on
earth — land or sea — the world wouldn't stop? The
winds would blow and the tides would change and the
sun would shine and the rain would fall —"

"And birds and animals wouldn't have to worry
about being hunted or dying from acid rain."

"True. But what would be the point?" Miss Longley
came to the end of a row and wrestled with a flourish-
ing weed. "I'm sure the world was meant for people
to live in and take care of. If we can just remember
that. Anyway, I watched you rowing. I could see you
on the two further legs of your course. You and the
dinghy seem to work very well together."

53

"Thanks! Did you see Stomper rowing *Flashdance?*"

"Yes, out by the lighthouse. He doesn't handle the oars as smoothly as you do, but he might with more practice. How many weeks until the race?"

"Four. I'm going to Rowbery this Saturday and sign up. My grandfather's going to sponsor me. After you pay me today, I'll have enough money for the entry fee."

"Why do they have an entry fee for a simple little race in the harbor?"

"Have you been to Rowbery in the last few years to see the races?"

"Not if I could help it. The traffic is usually abominable." Miss Longley felt there should be quotas on tourists and condominiums, and the Rowbery-Annisconset area had already filled its quotas.

"You've missed something!" Alec felt sorry for her if she thought the Annisconset Sea Fest was the tops in summer excitement. "There are races for three days. First the heats for the races, and then the finals. There are people from all over who anchor their boats around the harbor and have parties and cheer the races. There are people lined up along the Esplanade and in the park up on the Headlands. They bring beach chairs and all-day picnics. There's balloon men and those guys with umbrellas over their carts — the ones that sell hot dogs and ice cream and slush and fish and chips and tacos."

"Tacos! Mexican food in New England?"

"Sure! They're great."

"Amazing. It does sound like a — what do they call

it? — a media event? a tourist event?"

"And there's T-shirts. Like this one." Alec stuck out his chest to show ROW FOR IT printed over the Rowbery city seal.

"So for your entry fee you get a T-shirt?"

"Of course. But not like this. This one sells year round to promote Race Week."

"Ah, the wonders of the Chamber of Commerce. Well, keep me informed. I shall want to go and watch how you and my dinghy do. But I shall take my own beach chair and my own lunch."

Alec felt good about Miss Longley's planning to watch him race. He knew his grandfather and mother and Jeannie and Christopher Elvis would, too. But he wondered about his father.

He wanted to get the confession about the watch over quickly, so he sat on the back steps, waiting for Mr. Mott to come home. The sun pierced its way into the back yard. During the afternoon the weather had become hotter — hot even in Flounder Cove, where there were often breezes in summer and mists and fog patches in winter that missed Rowbery.

Alec's mother came out in her bathing suit. She lit the barbecue. "It's too hot to cook inside. Will you keep an eye on the grill while I whisk down to the cove for a plunge? I'll be on the rocks at the near end of the breakwater. On the ocean side. Jeannie's still playing down there. Want to come along and cool off?"

"I'm waiting for Dad."

She gave him an approving and loving pat on the shoulder and left. When his father arrived a little later

Alec felt queasy — partly from the fumes of the charcoal lighter fluid and partly from apprehension. Both Mr. Mott and his clothing looked limp from the heat.

"Have you got a minute?" Alec asked. That was what his mother usually said when Dad got home and she needed his attention.

Mr. Mott dropped his briefcase and jacket and tie on the steps beside Alec. "If it's a minute. Or two. I'm about to melt into the shower."

"Why don't you take a swim off the rocks? The ocean's great. Mum and Jeannie are there now. I'll go down with you." That wasn't what Alec had meant to say. And he hadn't intended to go right on and ask, "Why don't you ever swim? Or go out in a boat? We got water all around and you never go in!"

"You've noticed that, have you?" Mr. Mott pulled off his white shirt and tugged at the cotton T-shirt underneath that stuck to his body.

"Don't you know how to swim?" Alec suddenly felt sorry for his father, as if Alec and his mother knew how to do all the good things — swim and sun and row and tell silly jokes and play Yahtzee together — and Alec's father didn't know how to do anything but work and run.

"I swam a lot when I was your age. In a limestone quarry near where we lived. I never took you near one when you were growing up because they are so steep-walled and so deep. Over a hundred feet, most of them."

"I'm glad Mum taught me to swim at a pool!"

"She began when you were just a baby. She wanted you to be a good swimmer and you are."

"Were you as good a swimmer as you are a runner?"

"I never had one of those smooth mechanized-looking crawl strokes, but I was a strong swimmer. Or thought I was until a friend of mine got in trouble."

"What happened?"

"The summer I was thirteen, I was swimming with a friend my age, Bill Polanski. Each year we'd been diving from ledges higher and higher above the water. I had just stopped being scared each time I dove from a ledge thirty feet above the water. Then Bill insisted on trying the next ledge up — about ten feet higher. I climbed with him but I said it was his idea — he had to go first. So he said, 'Cluck, cluck, you chicken,' and made a silly face. I think he meant to jump feet first. But he slipped and he took a terrible plunge that wasn't a dive and it wasn't a jump and it took him into the water at a terrible angle. He didn't come up and he didn't come up."

Alec felt his heart beat faster, yet he couldn't really imagine how frightened his father must have felt, perched on a ledge forty feet above the water. Scared to jump and scared not to.

"What did you do?"

"Yelled to some kids swimming at the other end — and then I dove. Somehow I thought if I dove it wouldn't splash as much and I'd be down deeper and I would be able to see Bill and grab him."

"Could you?"

"No. I dove down deep, but I lost my breath when I hit the water. It was a terrible shock, hitting the water. I remember it seemed like breaking a pane of glass with my hands and then with my chest. It couldn't have been a good dive. I was stunned but I knew I had to turn myself around and up, but it was like hauling myself up hand over hand. I thought I was going to drown. Then when I finally surfaced I realized I'd seen something before I started to struggle up. Way under the water I'd seen what looked like a hand, reaching."

"Did anyone come to help?"

"The other kids came. I told them and we all began to dive and look. Each time I stayed under until my breath gave out. And each time was like climbing a rope to come up for air. I found later that I'd torn the cartilage in my shoulder."

"Did they find Bill?"

"Yes. They had to bring in scuba divers and underwater lights. They found him four hours later."

"He was drowned?"

"He was dead. The only consolation I had was that even if it had been his hand that I saw, I couldn't have saved him. He broke his neck. He died when he hit the water. There was nothing any of us could have done."

"Was that why you told me once — when I was playing with your stopwatch — that holding your breath for almost two minutes wasn't long enough? Because you'd been trying to stay underwater to find Bill?"

"Probably. Did Mum tell you that you could use my stopwatch for training?"

"Yes. But Dad, is that why you don't like to swim? Because of what happened?"

"It's my excuse. Actually the swimming part would be all right. It's getting my head underwater that's the hard part. I only do that in the shower. When I can turn the water off." Mr. Mott stood up. "Silly, isn't it!"

"I don't think so. I think you were very brave. Dad, I took the stopwatch before you said I could and it fell in the water and I got it out after a couple of minutes and I dried it off and I think it works now — but if it has any water stuck in it, it might not work later."

"I assume if it fell in the water, you had to fish it out."

"Right. It was midtide in the cove."

"Had to duck for it?"

"Right. I swam underwater to find it."

"Held your breath? Got your head wet?"

"Right."

"Good for you. That's more than I would have done to get it back. And now you know why."

"I'm sorry, Dad."

"It was a long time ago. But I can still feel every detail, as if it just happened."

"Mum doesn't know?"

"No. It's hard to tell someone you love about your failures."

"I won't tell."

"No need. Now we've talked about it, I can tell her.

I'm sure she never fell for my salt-water-itch excuse anyway."

"Dad, will you come watch me in the dinghy race?"

"I will be there. Cheering. From the shore."

8

Each day after he signed up for the race, Alec spent three or four hours rowing. He kept a chart and raced against his course record, trying to cut his time. Sometimes he was discouraged because it took him longer. More lobster pot buoys than ever bobbed into his way and the wake from lobster boats and speedboats set him rocking sideways so he'd lose his glide.

But there were a few mornings when the sea was calm and Alec found the lobstermen had been out earlier and the kids who hyped the speedboats in and out of the cove were lazy and came out later. Gradually he and the *Miss L.* improved until he could complete the course ten minutes faster than when he first began. He also set himself some distance goals to build up his endurance, and rowed several miles along the shoreline.

One day he took his mother and Jeannie and Christopher Elvis as far out as Blackberry Island for a picnic and swim. It was a little island about half a mile offshore.

When he told Miss Longley about his, she asked if

he'd take her. "It's been years since I went to Black-berry Island. And the berries must be ripe about now."

"Do you want to go tomorrow? About noon? That's the best tide."

"I'll bring the lunch."

At breakfast Alec told his parents he was taking Miss Longley in her boat for a picnic on the island. Mr. Mott looked at Alec's faded T-shirt and dirty cut-offs. "Is that what you're wearing to take Miss Longley out for a picnic?"

"Sure. She won't mind. It's what I wear to weed her garden. What do you think I should wear?"

Mr. Mott laughed. "Oh — a blue flannel blazer and long white trousers. It's just that I somehow expect Miss Longley to wear a picture hat and a high-necked blouse and a long skirt and to carry a parasol. She'll hand you a smart wicker hamper that will have knives and forks and spoons placed in slots under the lid. And you'll have cold chicken and cucumber sandwiches and lemonade and iced tea and walnut cake. And she'll have a book of essays to read while she sends you off to collect rocks and feathers and birds' eggs and sticks of driftwood."

"Dan! You're fantasizing about women one hundred years ago!" Mrs. Mott laughed. "Underneath that white shirt and tidy tie of yours there beats an extraor-dinarily romantic heart!"

"She won't dress up. We're going to pick black-berries," Alec said.

"I want to go, too," Jeannie announced. "Christo-pher Elvis has been very naughty and I want to go

62

away and leave him all alone in a closet and have some time to myself."

"What TV programs has she been listening to!" exclaimed Mr. Mott.

"I think it was something she overheard in the supermarket," said Mrs. Mott.

"She can't come," said Alec. "This is Miss Longley's picnic, not mine."

Mrs. Mott gave Mr. Mott his brown-bag lunch — a salami sandwich, a diet Coke, and a bunch of grapes — and sent him off with a kiss. She suggested to Jeannie that they put Christopher Elvis in the baby seat in the back of the car and drive to Boston to the Aquarium.

"Hey!" Alec objected. "I thought we were all going to do that together someday."

"We will," his mother promised. "Some rainy day when you're not training. It's just that Jeannie and I like to do things together, too. The Aquarium's good for more than one trip."

Alec sighed. It was hard to train every day. He hadn't spent a morning fooling around with Scooty since he'd started his program. Twice he'd asked Scooty to go out with him and hold the stopwatch and time each leg of the course and Scooty had. But yesterday Scooty'd said, "It's no fun watching you sweat. I'd rather hang around the cove and see what's going on." A little later Alec almost lost his grip on the oars as a powerboat whooshed out through the gap in the sea wall, gouging a trough in the water and a rough wake that thrust the *Miss L.* into a violent pitch. "Ya-hoo!" screeched the two boys lying on the deck over the cabin. "Ya-hoo!" Alec saw it was the Gateses' speed-boat with Stomper's older brother at the controls and Stomper and Scooty waving and yelling at him. He'd never make up the time he'd lost, sitting there with the dinghy wallowing like that, so he rowed back, and he'd felt cross and uncomfortable for the rest of the day.

Today when Alec arrived at the cove some girls were on the jetty. They were jumping off, trying to see who could make the biggest splash. Nancy Wentworth danced up and down on the stones, tossing her head and trying to shake water out of her ear.

"Hi," said Alec. He'd noticed that she'd been hanging around the cove. He hoped it was because she wanted to see him.

"Oh, hi," said Nancy.

"Got water in your ear?"

"What else!"

Alec felt stupid. He should have thought of something special to say. If he hadn't made plans with Miss Longley, he could have asked if she'd like to go out with him while he trained. He'd let her hold the stopwatch. Nancy went on jigging up and down. Alec didn't seem to be one of the reasons for her hanging around the cove.

He brought the dinghy over to the float and sat in it, picking at a new blister on his palm. He wondered if it was really worth it—all this hard work. What would he have to show for it if he won? He could get another T-shirt and his name in the paper just by paying the entry fee. His family and Miss Longley would tell him how great he was even if he just finished the course. Stomper didn't seem to be taking the race seriously. There he was again today, playing around in the powerboat while *Flashdance* floated at the mooring. And there were the girls swimming out to the power-boat. Stomper put the ladder out so they could climb aboard. Nancy was the first one up the ladder.

Perhaps if Alec's grandfather hadn't continually been checking on him, asking how his timing was coming along and whether he felt stronger and could row longer every day, Alec would have let up on himself a little. He'd asked his grandfather to watch what was going on in Rowbery Harbor and Old Lob reported that there were older fellows out every morning, training for the dory races. Those were the heavy boats rowed by two-man teams that took the races seriously because they were now international competitions. Ports in Nova Scotia and Newfoundland sent teams to compete, and this year there was an entry from France and another from Ireland. Rowbery's Race Week was becoming famous. There were rumors that a network TV crew would come to film it.

"Do you need a Band-Aid over that blister?" Miss Longley asked. Alec was startled. He hadn't heard her come down the gangway onto the dock. She didn't look like his father's fantasy of a gentlewoman of the 1880s about to embark on a proper outing. She didn't look like the Miss Longley who usually wore shirtwaist dresses, cardigan sweaters, and low-heeled shoes as she made her daily rounds of Annisconset activities, either. She wore a sportfisherman's cap with a long bill to shade her nose, a rather large long-sleeved khaki shirt and large khaki trousers pleated in at the waist by a leather belt. She wore stout boots. She carried an insulated picnic bag, a gallon Thermos, and a canvas duffel bag with a drawstring top. "All set to go?"

Alec helped her stow the picnic gear. "You want to sit in the stern or the bow?"

"If I sit in the stern, we'll bump knees. I'll take the forward seat."

So there they were, sitting back to back — he facing the stern and rowing forward and she facing the bow and telling him when he got off course — as they headed for Blackberry Island. Alec was relieved when she didn't say much. She seemed fascinated by the many summer cottages set in green lawns above the rocks that rimmed the shore. "How things have changed," she told him. "When I was a girl there were only four cottages between the cove and the lighthouse. The rest was left to trees and bayberries and poison ivy. And the rocks were covered with sea gulls, not sunbathers."

Alec concentrated on rowing. He didn't want to catch an oar in a pot line and give her a cold shower. He felt as if he were conveying an empress who was surveying her realm. He was relieved to reach the island without spilling her overboard or even splashing her.

She didn't wait for him to ask her to tie up at the abandoned dock. She flipped the end of the boat's line as easily as if she were tying her shoelaces. "There's a knot I've never forgotten. And when we're ready to leave, it will slip out like magic."

"Could it work itself loose? I mean, the tide will be starting down in half an hour and the boat could tug the line a lot."

"It will be fine. Now, shall we eat first and pick berries later? Or vice versa?"

Alec wanted to eat right then. His early morning row had created a hollow in his stomach. But it was Miss Longley's party. "Whatever you like."

"I was brought up on the reward system. Work first. Reward later." Then she noticed Alec's disappointment. "However, I'm sure we would enjoy picking berries more if we had some energy." She opened the insulated bag and pulled out two small packages. "Trail mix. Very good for you."

She tucked her package into her shirt pocket, adjusted her cap, and hung a large coffee can with a rope handle over her arm. She put another can out for Alec. "Did your mother ask you to bring back some berries?"

"No. But my father did."

"Good. We'll pick for an hour. Have our picnic. And then head back. I have an appointment at four."

Blackberry Island was long and narrow — about half a mile long and perhaps a quarter of a mile wide in a few places. In the middle were high ridges of ledge with some trees growing up from pockets of soil. The wild blackberries grew tangled in the flatter places between the ridges and the rocky shoreline. There were several places where boats landed, and on a nice summer day, more than one group of people might be berrying, picnicking, or swimming here and there.

Alec and Miss Longley set out into a berry patch together, but he soon discovered their methods of picking were different. With her long sleeves and long pants and boots she could work her way into the midst of the tangles without being scratched. And she was patient. She'd beat back a little space and stand in it and pick every berry in sight before moving on.

Alec, with his bare arms and legs, could only reach into the edges of the tangles without being scratched. So he moved on frequently. Occasionally he pitched a handful of trail mix into his mouth. At least the raisins in it were tasty. He worked his way around a point of land and out of Miss Longley's sight. When he had enough berries for a blackberry shortcake, which was what his father wanted, but not enough for jam, which his mother definitely did *not* want to make, he carefully put his can down by a rock. He was hot and he knew that on the other side of the island there were flat rocks where he'd picnicked with his mother and sister. It was a good safe place to take a quick swim. He climbed the ridge and crossed the bit of meadow where the tough grasses tickled his legs. He heard voices. Familiar voices. It was Scooty and Stomper.

Alec crept along until he could hover behind a rock and hear what they were saying. It really bothered him that Scooty, who had been his best friend ever since he'd lived in Flounder Cove, was spending so much time with Stomper. And when Alec peeked farther around the rock and saw that the *Flashdance* was swinging at anchor about twenty feet away from the shore, he was furious. If Scooty hadn't wanted to spend time with Alec in the *Miss L.*, why was he out with Stomper in the *Flashdance?*

It was a lonely business, training for a race. Now Alec felt not only lonely but abandoned! What kind of a summer was it when you lost your best friend to your best enemy — and ended up spending your time either with an old lady or working like a galley slave at rowing a boat?

Scooty and Stomper weren't talking about anything in particular. Alec hesitated, trying to decide whether to pounce out at them or to surprise them by swimming out to the *Flashdance* and pretending he was going to row off and leave them on the island. He thought of Stomper's dumping the fish guts into the *Miss L.* and of Scooty's abandoning him. He decided to swim out and board *Flashdance*. He could slide into the water farther along the shore.

He backed off silently and hurried so fast through the meadow that he ran through several patches of poison ivy. Then, just as he was tying his sneaker laces together so he could hang them around his neck while he swam, he heard two splashes. Scooty and Stomper had hit the surface with racing dives and were headed for *Flashdance*. From this far away Alec couldn't beat them to it. He sat down on a rock, totally disgusted.

He didn't want the boys to see him. But they did. They rowed close to where he sat. Alec noticed that Scooty didn't want to give him a direct look. But

Stomper was his usual self. "Hey — want to race? I'll show you how much I'm going to beat you by at Rowbery. Where's your little-old-lady-dinghy-thingy?"

Alec decided not to let them see how mad and hurt he was. He tried to stay cool. "Sorry, Stomp. Some other time. I'm busy."

"Busy doing what? Counting barnacles?"

"None of your business." For some reason Alec didn't want to say he'd brought Miss Longley to the island. But he wanted to convince them he was busy — full of plans — and didn't need them. Yet what would someone be doing, sitting all alone on a rock, gazing at the ocean? What had that fellow on the TV drama said as it showed him silhouetted against a flaming sunset? Alec remembered and quoted, "I'm meditating. I'm getting in touch with myself."

That made Scooty's eyes contact his in surprise, while Stomper fell over his oars laughing. He should have known Stomper would misunderstand what he said. Now he'd have even more to live down. What a rotten, rotten day!

He sat there pretending to meditate as Stomper pulled the boat away and with strong, steady sweeps of the oars sent the *Flashdance* almost shooting over the surface.

As soon as *Flashdance* was out of sight, Alec slid into the water. He loved swimming almost as much as he used to love rowing. He took a deep breath, put his face in, and with shallow kicks made his way out over the seaweed-covered rocks to deeper water. He liked the tingle of the salt. As he was alone, he didn't swim too far out, but he stayed in long enough to feel better. There was something calming about the rhythm of swimming, about the breathing and the stretched-out feeling of his limbs in the water.

When he came out he realized Miss Longley's hour for berry picking must be up, and he'd eaten up all his trail mix. He'd just stuck his sneakers on when he heard Miss Longley calling him. She stood on the ridge. "Stay there. I brought the lunch. I remembered this swimming spot and thought you might be here. Famished?"

Famished was a word Alec didn't know, but if it meant hungry, he certainly was. He helped her down onto the flat rocks and they made quick work of the lunch. What was it his father had predicted? Cold chicken, cucumber sandwiches, lemonade, iced tea, and cake? Miss Longley brought two submarine sandwiches — each filled with spicy cold cuts and cheese and peppers and tomatoes — and cold cans of Coca-Cola. And fresh peaches. Not bad, thought Alec. Not bad at all. He grinned at Miss Longley. "Thanks!"

"You are indeed welcome, Alec. I don't know why I hadn't thought of a picnic out here weeks ago. My brothers tented here one summer. They wouldn't let me stay with them, but they depended on me to bring them water and food every day or two. They pitched a tent right at the top of that meadow. What a happy time we had —"

"Do they live around here now?"

"No. They were both killed in the Second World

71

War. One in the navy. One in the air force. I'm the last of five generations of Longleys to live in my house. Now — have we left any litter? Not a crumb. Good. You know, I'd like to try rowing back."

On the way Alec picked up his can of berries. They rounded a point of land and came within sight of the old dock.

"Where's the boat!" Alec and Miss Longley said the words at the same moment.

The *Miss L.* was not there.

9

"Can you see her anywhere?" Alec asked. Since Miss Longley was a foot taller than he, perhaps she could see farther along the shore.

She stepped up onto a rock and looked in both directions. "No. The boat was at the dock when I took the picnic things and went to find you. I don't see how she could have come untied."

"Could that knot you used have worked loose?"

"A half hitch? Not in such calm water. It would take a really strong tug to pull it out."

Alec climbed up beside her. "I wish I had some binoculars."

"Of course! How forgetful of me. Hand me that duffel bag, please."

Alec saw the canvas bag resting next to her can of blackberries and got it for her. From it she produced a bird book, a tube of sunscreen, a towel, a pair of white rubber slippers —"In case I wanted to go wading," she explained — and a pair of binoculars. She scanned the horizon and the shore again. "No *Miss L.*"

Alec took a turn with the glasses and he looked for

Flashdance. He respected Miss Longley's nautical experience enough to believe her half hitch wouldn't have unraveled without help. He hadn't told Stomper and Scooty that he'd brought her out with him. He thought of the impulse he'd had to tease them by seizing their dinghy and rowing off. If they thought he was alone on the island they could also have thought it a big joke to untie the dinghy and strand him. Stomper might, anyway. Scooty, he hoped, would at least make Stomper tow the *Miss L.* safely back to Flounder Cove.

"I told Mum and Dad where we were going," Alec said. "When I don't come home for supper, they'll start looking."

"Perhaps my dentist will try to find out why I am not in his chair at four. Or more likely he will just charge me for the time."

She seemed calm, Alec was relieved to note. Not frightened of being stuck on the island, but simply adjusting to the situation and making the best of it.

But he didn't feel calm, especially if the boys had just let the dinghy go. The *Miss L.* could be on her way to Spain! He tried to remember Salty Ferris's remarks on the best places between Flounder Cove and Rowbery to look for driftwood. "That's where the current and the tides pile up the most stuff year-round," he'd said when Alec asked where his best chance of finding an abandoned boat might be.

But the tide was going out, not in. The dinghy would be pulled away from the shore, not pushed toward it.

And if the boat really was lost, he was out of the race. That made him even more sure that Stomper had purposely set *Miss L.* adrift. He needed to get off the island as quickly as possible and find out what had happened, maybe start a search for the boat.

"Did you notice any people around when you were picking berries?"

"No," said Miss Longley. "I was quite happy to think we were alone here. No intruders. Almost the way it used to be for my brothers and me. But we can run up a distress signal and you could climb to the ridge and look around and see if anyone else has come out for a swim or a picnic."

She reached into her bag and pulled out a brilliant orange plastic poncho. "How's that for a distress signal?"

"Great. What are we going to tie it on?"

"That's your department. You'll have to find something." She gestured toward the shore and Alec went scrambling along the tide line, looking for a long stick of wood. As he climbed up and over and down and around rocks and in and out of the twiggy bushes and high grasses, he realized how much poison ivy there was. He wished he'd worn long pants. Losing the boat was the worst thing that could happen to him, but breaking out in poison ivy would be second worst. Three years ago he'd had a bad case and his mother had warned him to be wary of it in all seasons. "Too bad it's an evil fact of life around an otherwise heavenly place."

He suddenly realized that Stomper also seemed to be an evil fact in his life. Alec usually went out of his way to avoid Stomper, just as he avoided poison ivy. Yet Stomper seemed to give him a year-round itch. And what had he ever done to Stomper except move into his neighborhood? Alec stood still and scratched. "Yah!" he yelled. "Yah! Yah! Yah!"

He saw people on a sailboat some distance away. He waved and yelled, "Help! Come pick us up!" They waved and went gliding on the same tack. His words hadn't carried that far.

He didn't find any long sticks at the tide line, so he climbed to the wooded ridge and looked for a brittle branch on a pine. If he hung on it, his weight might break it off. He jumped for one and clung. The bark grated against his fingers. He wiggled and swung until he heard a creak and then bounced until the branch snapped and came off the trunk, tumbling him into a bayberry bush. The limb was taller than he. It would be fine for flying a signal. He walked the ridge and looked along the outer shore of the island. No boats. No people.

Miss Longley saw him coming with the tree limb over his shoulder. "Perfect! Now, how shall we put the pole up?"

That was a problem. They had nothing to dig a posthole with and no way to pound a hole in a rock.

"Look!" Alec saw a way to do it. "We can tie the post onto that railing on the dock. If we just had something to tie it with." He didn't dare suggest using the leather belt that held up Miss Longley's large trousers.

"We'll rip up the towel." From her bag Miss Long-ley produced the towel and an ivory-handled fruit knife. They slashed and ripped the towel into strips, tied up the limb, and put the poncho over it so the hood was tied over the top and the brilliant signal flapped in the breeze. Alec watched how the wind slid over the sea, pleating the water into little tucks and ruffles.

From her bag Miss Longley also produced two oranges and two pears. They sat on the dock, swinging their feet and enjoying the soft sunlight. Alec spit the orange seeds out as far as he could.

"Are you having a good summer, Alec?"

Coming from Miss Longley, the question startled him. Especially since he'd been thinking about that very thing. About whether he was foolish to have put his whole vacation into wanting a dinghy, getting the use of one, and training so much and so hard for just one thing — to win a race.

"I'm not sure."

She didn't look surprised. "That's good."

"What do you mean?"

"Just that if you're not sure, it means you're willing to think about what you've been doing, training so hard. Whether you really want to be willy-nilly fol-lowing a routine, day in and day out, like a robot. Robots don't have much fun."

"Not even with all that zizzing about?"

"Certainly not. They're only doing what some master has programmed them to do. They don't ques-tion why they're doing it or what it means. You are.

77

That's sensible. You know I wouldn't have loaned you the dinghy, Alec, if I hadn't thought you were a reliable, resourceful young man."

"But the dinghy's gone!"

"Through no fault of yours. And see how resourceful you were to break off that pine bough." She handed him a pear and peeled another for herself with the ivory-handled fruit knife. From the way the drawstring bag now lay crumpled on the dock, Alec knew there was nothing left in it but the bathing shoes, the sun lotion, the bird book, and the binoculars. No more food. Neither of them spoke for a long time.

The sun bloomed in size as it approached the horizon. It suddenly seemed as huge and as hard and as red as the plastic floats that the fishing draggers carried to mark their nets.

Miss Longley stood up and reached out to her arm's length. She turned her hand sideways so that the width of her three middle fingers seemed to measure the distance between the bottom of the sun and the smudge of the horizon. "Three quarters of an hour till the sun sets."

"How can you tell?"

"Fifteen minutes for the width of each finger above the horizon. My brothers taught me that."

Alec glanced at his digital watch. It said 7:15. The tiny numbers weren't dramatic, like three finger widths to the horizon. But they emphasized how long he and Miss Longley had been on the island and how soon it would be dark.

"I hope Mum and Dad are checking the cove and

finding out that the *Miss L.* hasn't come back and they start looking for us."

"Oh dear! This will be more frightening for them. We know we're all right but they don't."

When the sun reached down to a finger's width of sky above the horizon, it was so dazzling Alec could only glance at it quickly.

Miss Longley said, "I've always liked the fact that Annisconset does stick its long neck into the bay so we can see the sun rise and set over water. Of course there's a smudge of hills on the other side of the bay. But with a sunset like this you can't see the hills for the brilliance of it all. And . . . there . . . it . . . goes."

As they watched, the edge of the bright disk seemed to dip into the water. Alec thought there ought to be a huge splash. It ought to make waves. But it was silent and faraway and soon it would be dark. Except for the buzzing of the mosquitoes and the occasional *su-su-slurp* of little waves against the dock, there were no sounds. Even the gulls had settled in for the night.

"That poncho isn't going to do us any good as a signal in the dark," said Miss Longley. "And I defy a mosquito to bite through it. You're going to need it over your bare arms and legs." They untied the poncho, and at her insistence, he put it on. Then they each settled into as comfortable a niche as they could find in the rocks by the dock. The afterglow's palette of reds and golds and purples faded to pinks and lavenders and blended into dusk.

"At last," said Miss Longley, "I'm spending a night

79

on Blackberry Island. It's something I've always wanted to do."

Alec laughed. There was something to be said for plans going awry. And making the best of it. That's where routine ran away and turned into adventure.

10

"Alec! Hey! Hey! Alec!"

Hearing his name nudged Alec out of drowsiness. He struggled to sit up. He'd forgotten the poncho and it was like trying to fight his way out of sleep and a straitjacket at the same time.

"Here!" he yelled. "Here — on the island. By the dock." It was really dark and all he could see were the red and green lights on a boat headed toward the island. He blinked as a searchlight was switched on and caught him in its beam.

"Oh, thank God!" That was his mother's voice. "Salty — we can tie up at the old dock."

"Right." Salty revved the lobster boat's motor and then let her drift in. Alec, free of the poncho at last, was on the dock and grabbed the line to tie her. His mother was out of the boat in a hurry to hug him. "Are you all right?"

"Sure. Everything's cool."

Miss Longley brushed herself off. "Hello, Mrs. Mott. I did not kidnap Alec. We were marooned."

"That's what we thought happened!" said Mrs. Mott. "Salty, would you CB back to shore and tell Pete that Alec and Miss Longley are okay? Dan is at the cove waiting to hear. Pete will tell him."

Alec heard the CB crackle as Salty gave the message.

"Did you find the dinghy drifting?" Alec asked.

"No. That would have been really scary! We didn't have to worry about your trying to swim to shore from a capsized boat. When you didn't come home in a reasonable time after supper, when it began to get dark, your father and I went to the cove. From the jetty we could see the *Miss L.* bobbing away at her mooring. So I dashed home to phone Miss Longley and see if you were at her house. When she didn't answer, then I did begin to panic. I couldn't figure out where you would have gone once you'd left the *Miss L.* in the cove. Or how the dinghy could be there when you weren't! I went running back to find Dan and thank heaven he was calm and logical."

"That's Dad!"

"There I was, ready to call the Coast Guard, and your father was sure we should look in the *Miss L.* first and see if she could tell us anything. Salty turned on a big spotlight and we had flashlights. When we pulled the dinghy in from her mooring, Dan spotted the note right away."

"A note? Someone left a note?"

"And I was only joking when I said that I hadn't kidnapped Alec!" exclaimed Miss Longley.

"It was on the stern seat, held down by a stone. Printed with purple Magic Marker letters. 'LOOK ON BLACKBERRY ISLAND.'"

"Scooty wrote it!" Alec was sure about that because Scooty was a Magic Marker freak. He kept one in his pocket, handy for drawing a symbol he'd made up and liked to leave in odd places. He'd heard about soldiers in World War II writing "Kilroy was here." He wanted people to know that William Herbert Arthur Merrill was here. Then he got to worrying about whales as an endangered species. What if people needed to be reminded that whales had been around, too! So he began by printing his initials — WHAM — and later added an exclamation point and drew the outline of a whale around the letters.

He liked to use purple or blue or black markers. The indelible kind. Alec knew Scooty spent hours looking for secret places to leave his mark. There was one under Alec's front porch. It made him feel so much better to realize his friend hadn't abandoned him completely, that Scooty cared about him enough to write a note.

"How do you know Scooty wrote it?"

"Because Scooty always keeps a marker on him and he was with Stomper on the island when they saw me. I think Stomper wanted to scare me by taking the boat.

Maybe he even wanted to set it adrift. But Scooty must have talked him into towing it in. I'll bet he didn't tell Stomper he put a note in the boat, either."

"I'm surprised no one saw the boys towing the boat or rowing it into the cove," said Miss Longley.

"Probably someone did. If we'd raised an alarm and started a search, I'm sure that would have been reported quickly."

Salty helped Miss Longley aboard. Alec handed in her bag and the cans of berries and jumped on. But as he slipped the line and pushed the boat away from the dock, he asked Miss Longley, "Did you really want to stay on the island overnight?"

"I did. And I didn't. Staying would have filled a wish I made years ago when it seemed an exciting thing to do. But sleeping on a rock is a hard way — now — to do it. I'm rather looking forward to a hot bath. And a softer bed."

Alec looked forward to seeing Scooty the next day and trying to find out what made Stomper take the boat. Had he done it because he was just plain mean? Or on an impulse — without thinking out the consequences? Alec didn't know Stomper well enough to figure that out. You didn't get to know someone you were always avoiding.

*

It was several days before Alec caught up with Scooty. In spite of having left the note, Scooty didn't come looking for Alec. Maybe Scooty had found he didn't enjoy being with Stomper all that much, but he didn't want to admit it.

When they did meet, it was at the cove. Scooty was carrying a rod and a bucket. Alec was tying up the *Miss L.* after doing his course twice. He was ready for a cooling-off plunge.

"Hey, Scoot! Want to swim?"

"I'd rather fish." Scooty concentrated on balancing over the tumbled rocks by the ladder without dropping his rod or the bait bucket.

Alec climbed the ladder. He tried again. "It's hot. A swim would be great. Come on."

Scooty hesitated.

"I'm not mad at you. If you hadn't left that note, I would have been stuck on Blackberry Island with OldMissLongley all night!"

Scooty put down the rod and the bucket and scrambled back over the rocks. The boys climbed the sea wall and walked on top of it toward the shore. Eventually the wall slanted to meet the ledges that stepped down to the water's edge.

"Yuck!" said Alec. "Low tide. Look at all that black slippery gunk on the rocks."

"The tide's turned. That's why I was going to fish. It's always better on an incoming tide." Scooty, showing the same confidence he had on his skateboard, walked quickly over the black gunk, shucked his T-shirt, and jumped in. Alec walked to the edge in a more cautious manner. You couldn't row with a broken arm or leg.

Suddenly he realized how the race affected everything he did or didn't do. He had as many things to be
careful about as a star pitcher or a concert violinist.

"I'll be glad when this race is over," he told Scooty.
They swam out toward the buoys on Salty's trap net.
The water felt wonderfully cool to Alec after his hot
work, and his body tingled from the massage the waves
gave him as he turned over and floated. Scooty floated,
too. Bobbing about, so relaxed, it was easy for them
to talk.

"I wouldn't have let you stay on the island overnight," Scooty said. "I was hanging around the cove.
If your Dad hadn't found that note I'd have told Salty
where you were."

"If you were there and you saw my parents going
nuts, why didn't you just tell them?"

"And have Stomper find out I did? He'd kill me. I
had to be able to defend myself — to be able to swear
to Stomper that I didn't *tell* your *parents* where you
were."

Alec understood. "What's Stomper got against me?
I only moved here four years ago. His family's got a
lot more money than mine. They've got a big powerboat. He's got a dirt bike. They bought *Flashdance* so
he could use it."

"He doesn't like you."

"I *know* that. Why?"

"Because you won the Pee Wee Rowers race the first
summer you were around here and then you went
around bragging about it. He said you were real

snotty — always talking about boats as if you knew all about them and you didn't even grow up here. He said you were a know-it-all pain in the butt."

"He went around saying all that to you and to other kids? He never said it to me."

"No. He just beat on you at the bus stop."

"Please. Don't talk about it. Maybe that's it, though. He can beat me up in a fight and be the big shot. But maybe I can beat him at rowing and that makes him mad. He's always got to win. No matter what."

"I think you've got it."

"So I just have to win that race and beat him that way." And, Alec added to himself, then maybe Nancy will see that Stomper isn't the greatest. She'll hang around with me.

Scooty said, "I'll be the timer when you train tomorrow if you want me."

"Great!"

Alec felt great, too, as he raced Scooty in to the rocks. His body felt strong and his legs and arms were doing exactly what he wanted them to. His mind was clear about why Stomper picked on him . . . he was a threat in the race. His friendship with Scooty was on again. He had nothing to worry about.

Except the weather. When he woke the next morning, the skies were dirty with black clouds and the wind whipped across the bay, flicking the waves into white caps. From his bed Alec could look out the window and see the weather without getting up. It looked so nasty that he curled up and went back to sleep.

The next time he woke, somebody was jabbing at him. He opened his eyes to find himself staring into two flat, unwinking blue eyes only inches from his own. A small hand kept on stabbing his cheek.

"Ye-ow!" Alec pushed Christopher Elvis away and sat up so quickly that he knocked Jeannie off the edge of his bed.

"Watch it!" She glared at him. "Christopher Elvis just wants to tell you Scooty's on the phone. You don't have to hit a little baby."

"You know he's not a baby. He's a DOLL."

"To you. Not me. You're mean to him because he wasn't a boat."

"Beat it," said Alec.

Jeannie hopped up onto the foot of Alec's bed and gathered Christopher Elvis safely into her arms. She sat there, grinning.

Alec leaned over until he could reach the cut-offs he'd dropped on the floor when he went to bed and wriggled into them under the bedclothes.

"Where you been?" Scooty asked when Alec got to the phone. "Jeannie said she'd get Christopher Elvis to wake you up. Did she have to go all the way to a cabbage patch to find him?"

"Probably. What's up?"

"Have you looked at the weather? Are you going to row today?"

"I saw. I don't think it would do any good. I couldn't make any time in that wind. One day off won't hurt."

"Want to go to Rowbery and hang out? My mother's

going shopping. We could get a ride over and take a bus back."

"Sure."

When Scooty's mother dropped them off, they wandered into the harborside park. Even on such a gusty, threatening day, the boys found a lot to watch. There still was a fishing fleet that used Rowbery for a port. A dragger which seemed to be flying a sail made of sea gulls above its deck thrummed along toward the pier where most of the fresh fish was unloaded. Another dragger tossed about at the ice plant, taking on the tons of ice it would need for a three- or four-day trip. Many boats couldn't afford to lay up during bad weather. An idle boat didn't earn anything. At the far end of the harbor were the freezer plants, huge concrete buildings with no windows, which rose up at the waterfront like fortresses. Alec liked to look for foreign boats unloading at the freezers — the enormous ships that came in from Iceland, Germany, Poland, and Portugal with blocks of fish already processed and frozen at sea into slabs. Sometimes boats from Japan were there, loading up. Alec had heard men on the streets in Rowbery speaking in languages he didn't understand, and once he'd found an Icelandic coin on the sidewalk. He and Scooty hung over the park railing and watched until it began to rain. Both boys wore foul-weather gear — waterproof parkas with hoods. As long as their heads and bodies were dry, they figured their legs, bare below their cut-offs, could take any amount of rain. They were used to cold slosh in their sneakers, since they fooled around in the cove so much. But after a while the rain seemed icy for summer and the wind made it worse.

"Let's go to my grandfather's," Alec said. "Maybe we can bum some lunch."

Old Lob was glad to see them. As Alec hoped, he was frying up some hot Italian sausages and he threw more into the pan for the boys. He sent Alec to get bread and macaroons from the Italian bakery across the street. Alec always enjoyed going there. The smell of fresh baking was inviting and the conversation in emphatic Italian was as exotic to Alec as the foreign boats in the harbor.

While the boys ate, Old Lob told them all he could about the upcoming races. "Maybe this year there'll be more tourists than come to see the Fiesta."

"Will they have a greasy pole?" Scooty asked.

"Would you try it if they did?" Alec wondered why Scooty wanted to do slippery things, like zinging around on a skateboard or trying to walk the length of a pole covered with grease just to capture the flag at the end.

"Sure! That would be great."

The greasy pole was one of the big events at the Fiesta in June, which led up to the Blessing of the Fleet — a rite so important to the fishermen and their families that the archbishop came to officiate. It was a four-day festival, with outdoor concerts and block dances, a carnival with rides and games; and in the crowded Italian section of Rowbery where Old Lob lived, the streets were colorful with arches of bright lights. By contrast, Rowbery Race Week had less of a carnival and more of an athletic atmosphere. The churches and the fishing fleet sponsored the Blessing and the Fiesta; the Chamber of Commerce and the stores and businesses sponsored Race Week. Each year they were trying to make it more eventful. This year they were stealing some of the Fiesta's excitement and putting on a greasy pole. "Hoping to make quite a splash with that!" Old Lob said.

Scooty wanted to go right over to the Chamber of Commerce and sign up.

"I'm not through eating." Alec was waiting for the pleasant burning sensation in his mouth and throat from the hot spiced sausage to cool enough so he could enjoy crunching into the macaroons, with their crispy outsides, melt-in-the-mouth insides, and intriguing almond flavor. The Palazzolas baked the best macaroons in the world.

Alec was really enjoying a day off from rowing and rowing and rowing and feeling hot and tired and hungry and thirsty. But he did want to know if Old Lob had any news about the competition. "Do you know how many signed up for the Junior Rowers race? And what about the kid who won last year — the one who was so big for his age and had hands about the size of a soccer ball?"

"You mean Skip Genovese? Or was that Tony Brosnan?"

"His name was Skip."

"You're safe there. He's turned thirteen. They got him entered in the Junior Varsity now."

"How old are the kids in Alec's group?" Scooty asked.

"Let's see. The groups start with the Pee Wee Rowers. They can be up to age ten. Then the Junior Rowers are ten through twelve. That's the group Alec and Stomper are in now. Junior Varsity Oarsmen are thirteen through seventeen. Anyone over that's a Senior Varsity Oarsman or in the International Dory competition."

"So there's some kids a year older than Alec he's got to race against?"

"Some," admitted Old Lob.

"And I'll be twelve in four weeks," Alec reminded them.

"Last I heard there were only eleven boats entered in the Junior Rowers. It's the little kids and the older guys who have the most entries."

"Do they have Race Week if it rains?" Scooty asked.

"Of course!" said Old Lob. "A little rain never stopped a doryman. That's what started these races, you know. Serious rowing competitions. Not tourist events. The only time in twenty-five years the races weren't held was one year when there was a hurricane threat and everyone around here either took his boat out of the water or had it tied up to shore as tight as could be."

"It better not hurricane this year!"

What a letdown that would be, thought Alec. All

he'd have to show for his summer's hard work would be how thin the seat of his cut-offs had become and how big his biceps and thighs were.

When he got up, his grandfather squinted at him. "Have you grown an inch in the last few weeks? Seems to me all that rowing is stretching you out."

"Could be!" Thinking that he had gained an inch gave Alec more confidence than ever. "I wish the race was tomorrow. I'm all ready to win."

~~~~~~~~~~~~~~~~~~~

11

"It's still raining!" Alec came down to breakfast three days later in a mood as heavy as the clouds. "I've got to row today. If I don't, my hands will soften up and I'll get blisters." It was the Monday before Labor Day Weekend. Four more days to the trial heats for the races.

"I hate to have you row on a day like this." Mrs. Mott was upset. "It's wretched out there. I'm sorry for all the summer people and tourists who are sitting around at great expense looking at the rain come down."

"What's the weatherman say?" asked Mr. Mott. "Are they predicting yet for this weekend?"

"It depends on who you listen to," said Mrs. Mott. "The Boston TV men are sticking their necks out and saying this weather system will be blown out to sea by Friday."

"With Labor Day Weekend coming up they wouldn't dare say anything else."

"But I like to listen to that radio station up in Portland. It always seems to me that weather around

Flounder Cove and Rowbery is more like what happens along the lower Maine coast."

"What do they say?" Alec asked.

"It's too soon to forecast the weekend. But they are predicting a big blow for tonight. And — the announcer and the weatherman were chatting after the forecast and they reminded fishermen and sailors that under all those clouds it will be a full moon. And also very high tide. So with a high wind, there could be some storm damage. When you check the *Miss L.,* Alec, be double-sure that she's bailed out and tied tight."

"Don't worry. I always do."

"Do you have to go out of the cove to row today?" asked Mr. Mott. "Couldn't you stay inside the sea wall?"

"I wouldn't get in much rowing. Most of the time I'd be paddling around other boats. In slow motion."

"Well — stick to the shore. And do watch the time so you aren't gone too long. Please." Mr. Mott picked up his briefcase. Ever since they had sat on the back steps and his father had told him about his friend's drowning in the quarry, Alec had felt a difference in how his father treated him — as if he were an adult, instead of a kid. Now he didn't order him to stay in the cove. He asked him please not to be gone too long — to consider the consequences and be sensible. It was so much easier to do that, than to be ordered *not* to do something and then feel he had to disobey.

When he went to the cove, a few men were around, carrying on with boat chores. Pirate Pete sat in his craft working on a cable to the controls. Despite the "continual drizzle and intermittent downpours" that Alec heard the Maine radio station forecast before he left the house, Pete looked comfortably at home and in his element. With his bald head and his great bleached beard, he reminded Alec of a picture in his book of myths of Poseidon, the Greek god of the sea. "This storm's been going on too long. Tears up the bottom, too. Look at those great clots of seaweed that got driven in. Looks like you could walk across the cove on 'em."

But Alec looked, as he always did, for the *Flashdance*. The boat wasn't at the mooring, or tied as a tender at the stern of the Gateses' powerboat.

"Is Stomper out training?"

"That's what he must be doing. Nobody'd be rowing for the joy of it today."

"How long's he been out?"

"Fifteen minutes or so."

"Alone?"

"Alone."

That meant Stomper at last was taking the race seriously enough to practice. "I'd better get at it," Alec said.

"Good luck. From the determined look on Stomper's face, you're going to need it."

Alec went to fetch the oars from Salty's shed, where he'd been leaving them. Salty was in a corner, sorting through a pile of junk. "Got to make more room to move in here," he muttered. "Some of this stuff wouldn't even go in a yard sale anymore." Then Salty turned to look at Alec. "Goin' out?"

"Sure. When's it going to stop raining?"

"Oh, two days, more or less. This time of year, once one of these northeasters gets going it takes time to get rid of it. And you better be prepared for some big swells to pull against in Rowbery even midharbor. The ocean can keep on bein' riled even after the wind and rain quit."

"Great!" Alec spit on his hands. "Maybe I ought to take some weight in the boat today and practice pulling real hard."

"Don't know as that will help you much. But if you want to try it, you could take some of this junk and then dump it for me out there before you come in. That way I won't have to bag so much for the trash collector. Seems they're too fussy to pick up anything these days that isn't all gift wrapped in plastic for them."

Salty pulled a bucket over and dumped in a collection of metal oddments. By the time Alec picked it up, he felt it weighed at least fifty pounds.

"Just bring back the bucket," Salty told him. "I swear there's a world shortage of buckets."

Alec trudged around the cove to the breakwater side and out along the roadway below the sea wall. He climbed through the tumble of rocks that blocked the road and put down the oars and the bucket by the top of the ladder. It was high tide so he only had to go down four rungs on the ladder to step into the dinghy, which was half full of rain water. He unlatched the lid of the stern seat and looked into the little space where he kept his bailer and a spare oarlock and some rope. The bailer, a large plastic Clorox jug cut into a scoop, was gone. Then he remembered. Late yesterday afternoon he'd bailed the boat out and checked her lines in a big rush because his father had decided to take them to the movies. He'd probably left the bailer in the boat and the wind had picked it up and blown it away. It was lucky Salty loaned him the bucket. He started to dump the contents on top of the stern seat and then decided some of the pieces might roll around and drop into the bottom of the dinghy while he was rowing. He opened the seat again and placed them inside. He'd dump them out before he went back in the cove.

The rain was only drizzling now. Alec bailed out the water that had collected in the boat. He hoped he could complete his training course without another downpour dumping more in. If he kept his slicker on, he'd be mighty sweaty. But if he took it off and his sweat shirt got soaked, he'd be mighty chilly. He decided to work up a sweat first. Then when he took the shirt off, he could think of the drizzle as a cool shower.

Once outside the gap in the breakwater he set off on the four legs of his course. He hadn't bothered to bring the stopwatch because he knew he'd be slow. Even this close to shore the wind shoved at the water and the water pushed at the boat in a direction he didn't want to go. The motion threw off the long stroke he'd been developing before the storm. He seemed to need shorter, deeper, jerkier pulls on the oars. And the oars seemed stubbornly to want to do something different, too. He was trying to figure out whether it was the four-day gap in his training, the added weight in the boat, or the strong push of the waves and the tide, when he saw the *Flashdance*.

Stomper was coming back on his usual route over to the lighthouse on Annisconset Point. It was a straight line course, and since most lobstermen now had their pots farther offshore, there were few obstacles like buoys. Stomper could work up a steady rhythm with the oars and get the most momentum out of his dinghy's motion. Alec wondered if he should have kept his training course that simple and gone for speed and momentum instead of adapting to the feel of four slightly different situations. But Old Lob told him the Junior Rowers race was over a four-legged course, and the tide and the currents in the harbor would push and pull a little differently on each leg.

Stomper came near enough to yell. "Want to race to the lighthouse and back?"

Alec hesitated. What if Stomper should beat him? That would be unbearable. He couldn't let that happen. He was just going to say, "I'll race you in Rowbery Friday," when Stomper added, "Don't bother! A boat named for a little old lady could never beat a boat called *Flashdance*. It's impossible."

"No, it's not!"

"Prove it!"

"Right!"

Then Alec realized Stomper had teased him into agreeing to race and that made him furious with himself as well as with Stomper.

Stomper pulled on one oar and circled the *Flash-*

dance around to start back on the course. Alec yelled, "Hey! I won't race if we don't start together. Wait till I get this slicker off."

Flashdance bobbed about as Stomper kept her more or less in one spot. Alec threw his slicker into the bow of the *Miss L.* He took a few strokes to pull even with the other dinghy, but with a good thirty feet between them. He wanted to let go of one oar and scratch his nose, but he didn't trust Stomper. "Let's count one, two, three together and start on three," he said.

Stomper didn't even say, "Sure." He just yelled, "One —"

"Two," Alec joined in.

"THREE!" Off they went and for the first four or five minutes the boats kept pace. Then Alec was dismayed to find Stomper edging ahead. *Flashdance* seemed to be winging over the water, while *Miss L.* trudged through it. Alec's arms already ached. Then he remembered the added weight. The boats weren't evenly matched. It was like a horse race with a weight handicap for certain horses. He wondered if he could reach into the stern seat and grab something out and heave it overboard. Probably not. He'd just have to row harder.

The course they were on actually made the longest leg of a triangle, with the shore providing the two shorter legs — one fairly short, and then the longer one jutting out to become Annisconset Point. Alec and the *Miss L.* were closer to the shore, with Stomper and the *Flashdance* going along some thirty feet farther out. After a while Alec realized Stomper was not only

100

pulling ahead but widening the distance between the boats. He was some fifty feet farther out now.

Alec wondered how close Stomper would go to the shore of Annisconset Point before he turned. It would be a complete reversal of direction — not the quick quarter turn Alec was used to making. He heard Stomper yelling back at him. "Go around the rocks with the *Danger: No Swimming* sign. Then start back."

That was fair enough. It was better than some imaginary turning point that Stomper suddenly picked in the water.

But was it? He looked over his shoulder and saw Stomper turning *Flashdance* to the left. He'd be swinging with the tide into the narrow channel between the knob of dangerous rocks and the shore. He'd race through with the current and then swing out to start back. Alec, who had been closer to the shore all the way, had two choices — both bad. He could swing to the right and fight through the channel against the current, losing time, or he could suddenly shift direction, row fifty feet out of his way, and take the channel the same way Stomper did. He'd lose time that way, too.

Maybe fighting the current wouldn't be as costly as the added distance. He'd try it, even though he knew the danger sign was there because at high tide the current raced through. Yet common sense (which seemed to arrive in his head in his father's tone of voice) said: Go the other way.

Alec spun about and rowed frantically out toward the bay. If he lost this race, it would be due to the added weight and the advantage Stomper had in using a course he knew well. So it wasn't a fair race. Not that Stomper would see it that way. But Alec would — just as he'd felt it wasn't fair the way the raffle ended up. Yet it was what happened that he had to deal with — fair or not.

As he reached a turning point and thrust the *Miss L.* toward the channel between the rocks and the shore, he was glad he hadn't tried to do it the other way. Over his shoulder he could see the surface water pulled into a moving pattern as inevitable as the treads on a tank. The rippling diamonds seemed to seize the dinghy and throw it along. The relief of not having to pull on the oars surprised Alec. He held them poised in the air, ready to steady *Miss L.* if necessary, while the current did the rest and then released the boat in a whirl of foam beyond the channel. Any other time Alec would have wanted to go back and do it again. He thought it was as exciting as white-water canoeing would be.

But Stomper was some hundred feet ahead of him and keeping up a steady pace. How could Alec ever catch up!

It was discouraging, but Alec settled down to a steady stroke. He found that his arms didn't ache anymore and some kind of automatic drive had taken over. Everything — his arms, his back, his legs, his breathing — worked together just as he'd trained them to do. Gradually he began closing the distance, especially when Stomper for some reason lost his grip on his right oar and boggled a few strokes, swerving off his course a bit. That helped, but Alec realized what helped most of all was the practice. Stomper, for all he was bigger and supposedly stronger, seemed to be getting tired.

They had started the race so quickly that they hadn't agreed on where to end it. When he got a little closer, Alec yelled, "First one through the gap wins!"

"Okay!" Stomper didn't waste his breath arguing. He was only about fifteen feet ahead of Alec, and Alec had managed so the *Miss L.* could pass the *Flashdance* on the shore side — closer to the entrance to the gap. That made up for Stomper's being in front. It looked like a neck-and-neck finish.

Then a large powerboat — the kind that seems to be a three-decker with picture windows as well as a fish-spotting pulpit — roared out of Flounder Cove. The man driving it paid no attention to the speed limit or the so-called "courtesies of the sea." The boat was *Old-Man-of-the-Sea* and she was off on one of her wild tours. What was it Pirate Pete called them? Power trips!

Alec tried to steer away from the powerboat's course as hard as he could. But suddenly she veered violently toward him. The man steering her must have seen *Flashdance,* but, at the same time, he had not seen the *Miss L.*

Old-Man-of-the-Sea was now on a direct course to crash into Alec.

It seemed to Alec that the powerboat loomed up at him like the great white shark in *Jaws.* Then at the last second, within two feet of the dinghy, it suddenly steered away. Alec had the impression of great white teeth arching over his head as the bow of the *Old-Man-of-the-Sea* roared past.

But while the huge boat's bow did miss the dinghy, her stern just ticked the *Miss L.*'s bow. It shoved her askew. Then the thrust of the powerboat's wake tipped the dinghy too far over.

The *Miss L.* capsized and Alec flew out into a whirl of churning sea.

12

It happened so quickly that Alec could barely understand why he was suddenly, shockingly, completely surrounded by water. It was in his eyes and his ears, up his nose and over his head. He kicked and treaded water. He reached out and grabbed water. His sweat shirt was heavy with water and his short rubber boots filled with water. Instead of his flailing arms pulling him toward the surface, his shirt and boots dragged him down. He needed air! His lungs were going to explode and then a flood of water would rush in.

The story of his father's friend — the boy who never came to the surface of the quarry — filled his mind. He had seen how his father still felt mad and sad about it years later. He couldn't let his father go through that again. He had to hold what breath he had left. He had to take off the sagging sweat shirt. He yanked at the zipper tag and tugged it down until the bottom of the shirt opened. He wriggled out of one sleeve and then the other. It dropped away. He felt lighter. He tried again to swim to the surface and saw, lowering toward him, an oar. Then he felt a burning pain in his lungs and throat and a bursting agony in his head. His sight seemed to dim. His hands drifted up and one touched the oar. He clutched it. He managed to bring the other hand to it, to clasp the oar and hold on.

Someone was bringing the oar up, pulling his body, hauling it like a big fish, to a boat. But he couldn't keep his mouth closed any longer. It burst open with a great gasp. He swallowed water and it choked him. At last his head rose above the surface. He kept gasping, now trying to refill his exhausted lungs. He clung to the oar, panting, shaking his head, flinging off drops of salt water and tears of fright.

"Hey! Mott! Take hold of the boat! You're going to pull me overboard if you don't let go of that oar!"

Alec was dazed but he managed to look up and focus on the person in the boat holding the oar. It was Stomper.

Seeing Stomper in the role of rescuer added to Alec's confusion. He couldn't let go his grip on the oar even to put one hand on the boat.

"Hey!" Stomper was yelling again, but louder this time, hoping someone in the cove would hear. "Hey! Help! Someone! Quick!" Realizing that Alec was in a kind of shock, Stomper crouched so he could brace the oar on the gunwale. But he couldn't reach Alec's hands at the end of the oar. It was going to take someone else to hoist Alec out of the water.

Alec gripped the oar in hands that might have been cast in bronze they were so immovable. He was still gasping and choking and not really looking at anything.

At last there was the sound of a motor and Pirate Pete's boat slid through the gap. He saw the situation and in seconds brought his boat close enough to kill the motor and drift.

"He was drowning!" Stomper said. "He capsized. He was under for ages. He can't get it together to grab the boat and I can't reach him."

"Alec!" Pete ordered. "Listen up! Here's a life ring. Grab it and I'll pull you in." He tossed the ring so it landed in front of Alec. "Alec — you've got to let go of the oar. Grab the ring. I'll count to three. One. Two. THREE!"

That did it. Alec let go of the oar, clutched the ring, and Pete pulled him to his boat, leaned over and hauled him onto the gunwale. Then he flopped him down into the boat. Alec still seemed stunned.

"Can you row back all right?" Pete asked Stomper.

"Yeah."

"I'll take Alec in. I think he's just scared but he could have gotten water in his lungs." Pete saw the *Miss L.* floating upside down about a hundred feet away. "See if you can tie *Miss L.* to a pot buoy so she won't drift. I'll get her later."

Pete whirred off. By the time he neared the dock in Flounder Cove, Alec had recovered his breath. He could see without blurs rolling in front of his eyes. But his throat and his stomach felt funny. He was still terrified by how close he'd come to drowning. He did not want to go in the water — even go out in a boat on the water — ever, ever again. He shivered at the memory of the water enclosing his head like a plastic bag. He leaned over the gunwale and threw up.

Pete tied up at the dock. Then he bent over and put his arms around Alec and held him close. "You're okay. You made it. In a couple of hours you'll feel fine again."

Alec tried to speak. "Stomper —" It hurt to talk and his voice was hoarse.

"Stomper what? He didn't capsize you, did he? He tried to save you!"

"He — did — save me," Alec whispered.

"Was it *Old-Man-of-the-Sea?* That guy gunned out of the cove like a rocket! Did the wake hit you? It would have been like a shock wave."

"The boat hit me."

"And he never stopped? Just kept on going?"

Alec nodded.

"The Coast Guard ought to know about that. He can be arrested for causing an accident. You're shivering, Alec. You've got to get those wet clothes off. How about it? Think you can walk home?"

A girl's voice called down from the gangway between the jetty and the dock. "We can take him. My mother's car is right over there. She's getting lobsters from Salty."

The gangway jounced as a figure in a green slicker jumped onto the dock. Alec recognized Nancy. He moaned. She had seen him throw up. This was, without a doubt, the most ghastly day of his life.

"I wasn't seasick," he rasped.

"He nearly drowned," Pete explained. "Can you get your mother right away?"

"She's in Salty's shed. Come on, Alec. We'll drive you."

Alec protested. "I only live up the street."

But when Pete set him down on the dock, Alec's knees gave way. He fell against Nancy and she had to hold him up while Pete finished securing the boat. Here Alec had been planning to do something spectacular — to beat Stomper by boat lengths in the race — so she would notice him. And here she was and he was soaking wet and couldn't even stand up. It wasn't fair! It was as topsy-turvy as his enemy, Stomper, being his rescuer.

"Let's go!" Pete picked up Alec. Nancy bounded up the gangway to get her mother. Alec felt woozy enough not to protest and he was glad when Pete got into the back seat of the car with him. Pete could tell his mother what had happened. Alec was too limp.

Mrs. Wentworth drove close to the back steps. Nancy banged at the door, and when Mrs. Mott came, Pete carried Alec in. The Wentworths promised to come back later and see how he was.

While Mrs. Mott stripped Alec's wet things off, Pete explained as much as he could. "It's Stomper who saved him. He'll give you the whole story."

"I want to see him for sure, to thank him and hear just what did happen. If you see him now at the cove, please tell him how grateful I am and I'll phone him later."

"I'll do that. Alec, do you think you swallowed much water?"

"I don't know. Maybe. I think I came up with my mouth open."

"Keep him warm," Pete said, "and if he gets a fever, maybe a doctor should check his lungs."

"Thanks, Pete. For bringing him in and all the way home. As soon as I get Alec into bed, I'll call Dan. He'll want to report *Old-Man-of-the-Sea*. How could any man be so careless! How could he leave Alec in the water like that!"

"He never looked to see, and his motor is so powerful, he couldn't hear either."

After Pete left and his mother brought him hot milk and tucked him up with extra blankets, Alec fell asleep.

When he woke, it was late afternoon. His father sat in a chair by the window. He had papers strewn over the foot of Alec's bed and he was writing on a pad of yellow paper. He'd brought his work home so he could be with Alec when he woke up.

"Dad —"

"Alec!" Mr. Mott let the papers flop to the floor as he moved to sit on the bed. He stroked the hair back from Alec's forehead and looked intensely into his eyes, as if he were trying to make sure Alec was still inside himself — that the fright his son had been through hadn't spirited him away. "That was a terrible thing to happen. But you're going to be all right."

"I was lucky Stomper was there." Alec's voice was weak. It still hurt to talk.

"Stomper stopped by a while ago. He and Pete brought the *Miss L.* in. Just the peak of the bow got broken. The powerboat barely ticked the *Miss L.*, but it was enough to throw you over. A bit closer and you'd have been completely run down."

Alec closed his eyes and shuddered. His father took his hand. "That's what *didn't* happen, thank God. The Coast Guard has an alert out to pick up *Old-Man-of-the-Sea* and investigate the accident. But that man won't ever get another mooring in Flounder Cove, that's certain!"

Mrs. Mott came in and handed Alec a glass of ginger ale. Alec took one look at it and handed it back.

"Too many bubbles." It reminded him of the wild whirl of bubbles stirred up by the powerboat's propeller as it churned past him when he was thrown in. His mother took it away and came back with apple juice.

"Miss Longley phoned. She said she'd have Ezra Elliott pick up the boat tomorrow and he could probably fix it in time for the race Friday."

"It doesn't matter. I'm not going to race."

"You're not? After all your hard work training for it?" Alec's mother was surprised. "You'll be fine by tomorrow. And then you'll feel differently, I'm sure."

"No. I don't want to be on the water or in the water ever again."

"Don't worry about that now," said Mr. Mott. "As

the saying goes, tomorrow is another day. Let it be for now."

"I mean it," said Alec.

He went downstairs for supper, but he didn't eat much. Swallowing was an effort. He talked to his grandfather on the phone. Mrs. Mott had called him to tell him about the accident, but Old Lob wanted to hear from Alec himself that he hadn't suffered any injuries. "You got your back in one piece and your fingers all working, and you can still row!" he cheered Alec on.

"Great," said Alec. He didn't tell his grandfather he wasn't going to race. He wasn't up to an argument.

Nancy and her mother came by with a half gallon of strawberry ice cream. That was easier to swallow. Alec and Nancy sat in the living room, spooning down the ice cream, while he tried to think of what to talk about. Mrs. Wentworth and his parents sat around the kitchen table, drinking coffee and discussing the accident. Salty Ferris and Pete also arrived. It was time, they felt, for the people who used Flounder Cove to put someone in charge of seeing that the regulations were posted and obeyed.

"Annisconset says we're too small for a harbormaster," Salty explained. "They won't pay for one."

"How about a covemaster?" asked Mr. Mott. "Think small and get things done."

"If we charged an additional fee for each mooring, we could pay a covemaster during the summer at least," said Pete.

Alec was relieved that Nancy didn't expect him to talk. He kept wanting to ask, "Did you see me throw up?" Yet he really didn't want to hear that she had.

Nancy talked. Did Alec know she'd been around the cove that summer? She liked to dive off the jetty at high tide. She had a red bandanna-print bikini. She had an orange bikini, too. She hated the cove at low tide. It stunk. But there were some great rocks to tan on at low tide. Did Alec like to lie around and get a tan? Did he row all the time? Did he know Dottie Perry? Did he know Dottie Perry thought Stomper Gates looked like Matt Dillon? Dottie was all excited because Stomper was such a hero.

Up to that point, Alec enjoyed listening. Nancy was paying attention to him, despite his appearance after the accident. She'd come back specially to see how he was doing. Then Nancy asked, "Don't you think Stomper is a hero?"

What could Alec say? He couldn't deny being rescued, but it was hard for him to see Stomper elevated to a hero's role. He wondered how long Nancy's interest in a victim would last.

"I can't wait to see Stomper and tell him how brave he is," said Nancy. She stared expectantly at Alec until he said, "Me, too."

But what was especially brave about keeping Alec from sinking while Stomper stood in a boat? Alec gave him that all right. But wasn't Alec the *brave* one to survive such a fright? Was that fair? When was Alec ever going to win one!

The news was getting around that people were meeting at the Motts' house to organize some kind of protest to the Annisconset Town Council about the lack of safety enforcement at Flounder Cove. A professor who moored his sailboat there came in, followed by Stomper and his parents and brother. Scooty's father phoned and said they'd be over in a little while. Mrs. Mott sized up the growing crowd and suggested that Alec and Nancy and Stomper enjoy their ice cream at the kitchen table, while the adults took over the living room.

Alec and Stomper sat across from each other and Alec found himself staring at Stomper as if he'd never seen him before. He'd always thought Stomper had a mean look — that his eyes blazed out with a leer and his mouth curled into a sneer — and that he never laughed without its seeming nasty. Alec had felt that way from the first day Stomper had called him a "squeaky squirt" and told him to wait to get on the bus with the little kids. Alec wouldn't give up his place and Stomper had pushed him and slapped him around. After that Alec didn't give in if Stomper started something, but he learned to avoid him as much as possible. It seemed as if most boys avoided Stomper. Dottie Perry and Nancy and the girls who hung around the cove must be the only ones who saw him in a different light.

Alec couldn't feel that the Stomper who always seemed to enjoy annoying people had really changed all of a sudden. It couldn't be like a fairy tale where a valiant deed by a monster turned him into a prince.

But he had to admit Stomper had been quick to reach the capsized dinghy.

"Could you see me underwater?" Alec asked.

"Not right away. That boat kicked up a real mess. It was like looking into a head of beer — froth all over. Then way down I could see you trying to get your shirt off and I was wondering whether to jump in and then try to get back to the boat with you. Or to stay in the boat and see if you'd grab an oar. So I tried the oar."

"Thanks," said Alec. "For doing it. For saving me."

"Well, you probably would have come up. Sometime." It seemed as if Stomper was trying to be modest. As if he felt enough of a hero not to have to gloat over Alec's misfortune. "I would have missed you, Mott. You're not a bad kid."

Not a bad kid! Alec felt a tremor of energy running through him. Who did Stomper think he was — besides a hero? Then he realized Stomper was grinning at him and it wasn't a sneer. He looked friendly.

"You're not a bad kid," Stomper repeated. "But I'm still going to beat you in the Junior Rowers race."

"You won't have to worry about that," Alec told him. "I won't be in the race."

"Your boat will be fixed in time."

"I heard. That doesn't matter. I'm not going to row."

Nancy and Stomper looked at him with disbelief and then with embarrassment. Alec didn't have to tell them he was afraid. They could see it, and they didn't know what to say to him.

13

Alec was sitting on the front porch the next morning when Ezra Elliott's truck went down to the cove. He watched it park on the jetty and Salty go over to speak to the driver. Together they loaded the wounded *Miss L.* into the truck. Alec had thought about walking down earlier to see the damage, but what was the use? He hadn't changed his mind about not racing. Even the thought of being out on the water in a dinghy made him feel queasy.

His father had left early for Rowbery. Mr. Mott was going to the Coast Guard station to file a complaint about the *Old-Man-of-the-Sea.* Alec's mother was stepping about the house, doing things as usual, but having a hard time not interfering with his decision. He knew she felt he was being silly — that later on he'd regret giving up the race. She must have said so to her father, because as Alec came downstairs for breakfast, he heard her end of a conversation with his grandfather. No, she did not want Old Lob to come over and give Alec a pep talk. Alec had to work this out for himself.

When Scooty came over after lunch, Alec couldn't explain how he felt to him, either. Scooty seemed to think that Alec had been through something that was very exciting. "Guess who called up Stomper this morning?"

"Dottie Perry."

"Who?"

"Some girl who thinks Stomper looks like Matt Dillon."

"She's a creep-o. He doesn't look like Matt Dillon."

"So who called up Stomper?"

"A reporter from the *Rowbery Enterprise*. He asked all about how Stomper rescued you. He sent a photographer down a little while ago to take his picture. And pictures of Flounder Cove. I went down and watched. The Coast Guard has a search on to locate the *Old-Man-of-the-Sea* for causing an accident, so it's news. Maybe they'll want your picture, too."

"Why? They don't take pictures of victims unless they're dead and they're being hauled off on those stretchers with wheels. Then some TV reporter sticks a mike in some relative's face and asks how it feels."

"Yeah. How do you feel about your son's drowning, Mr. Mott? How do you feel, Mrs. Mott?"

"I can tell you how they feel. Dad is mad at *Old-Man-of-the-Sea* and Mum thinks I'm a quitter."

"For dropping out of the race?"

"Right."

"Don't you feel okay now?"

"My legs and arms don't feel like they were stuffed with those plastic peanut things anymore and my throat isn't sore. But I don't know. Rowing around Rowbery Harbor and trying to beat ten other guys just doesn't seem that big a deal now."

"What if Stomper wins? You'd hate that."

"No, I wouldn't. If he wins, he wins. He won't bother me anymore."

"Why? You think he's any different because he did one good thing for a change?"

"No. He'll always be a pain in the butt to someone. But there wouldn't be any point in its being me."

"Why?"

"It's sort of like — he could have saved me or not. Like that Roman emperor on TV who did 'thumbs up' to save a guy and 'thumbs down' to kill him. Stomper decided to save me — so that's it. But first he had me just where he's always wanted me. Completely under his thumb. Now he doesn't have to bother with that anymore."

"Could be. You've had yours. Maybe I'll be next," Scooty said. "It's too hot here. Want to go swimming?" Scooty asked out of habit, without thinking of anything but plunging in from the rocks below the sea wall to cool off.

Alec went so far as to pretend to gag.

"Okay." Scooty got up. "You sit and sweat. I'm not going to."

He left. Alec sat for a long time, not even thinking, just kind of waiting for something inside him to go click and start another phase or another program. Like the dishwasher did when, after a prolonged hmmmmmmmmmm, it went CLICK and the dial sprang

118

forward a notch and water went thrashing into the machine, and the machine got on with its cycle. But nothing in Alec seemed to go click. He sat there, feeling his machine was broken.

Jeannie came out on the porch. She had on her swimsuit. She put Christopher Elvis down on the hammock and stripped off his diapers and forced him into a tiny pair of shorts. "We're going swimming. Want to come?"

"No."

"I need someone to baby-sit Christopher Elvis while I get wet."

"Take him in with you. You just put his suit on."

"You know he'd be ruined if I got him wet!"

"Then why do you pretend he's real! Put him in and see what happens. I don't know — if he floats maybe he is real. If he sinks, *tough luck!*"

"You're sick!"

"Creep-o!"

"Do I hear the dulcet tones of my two lovely children?" Mrs. Mott stood in the doorway with her terry beach robe over her suit. "How about it, Alec? You'd feel better if you even sat on a rock and cooled your feet in a tide pool. This is a real August heat-and-steam wave."

"I'd feel better if you all went off and left me alone."

"Then we'll do it," said his mother.

Some time later when the phone rang, Alec hoped it would be Nancy. She'd promised to call when she got back from shopping for school clothes with her mother. He knew he didn't have to worry anymore about what to say to Nancy. He just had to listen and say "uh-huh" now and then. That was all right. Nancy enjoyed talking. He didn't mind listening.

It was, however, his grandfather on the line. "I saw your friend Stomper Gates this afternoon, Alec. Told him I was pretty impressed with how he saved my grandson."

Alec felt a faint click. He was getting tired of hearing Stomper praised. "All he did was stick an oar in my face and then hold on to it while I hung on."

"But he really used his head. Lots of fellows would have jumped in and maybe drowned too."

"Maybe he didn't want to get wet."

"Anyway," Old Lob went on. "He was in at the Chamber of Commerce paying his entry fee for the race. He tells me you're dropping out."

"That's not news. Mum told you this morning."

"I thought maybe you'd changed your mind. I've scouted the Rowbery competition for you. There's only one fellow bigger than Stomper and he hasn't been training much. He's depending on being bigger. With all your workouts, I'll bet you could row rings around him."

"Maybe Stomper can beat him."

"What's with you, Alec? I thought you wanted to add the Junior Rowers trophy to that one you got for the Pee Wee race four years ago. I thought I had a real go-for-it grandson. Are you going to disappoint your poor old grandpa?"

"It looks that way. You know that old trophy? Well,

the gold paint's flecking off and you can see the plastic or whatever it is underneath. It's ugly, too."

"You didn't think so when you won it. It really meant something to you."

From where he sat in the living room, listening to his grandfather alternate between wheedling him into racing and goading him about not racing, Alec could see the trophy on top of a bookcase. It was a figure, stationed on top of a series of pedestals, that looked as if it had been adapted from a trophy designed to honor some other sport — golf, perhaps. Surely no serious oarsman would pose holding a symbolic oar so awkwardly. Alec remembered his father saying, "That's dreadful! Why don't they give the kids some beautiful model boats for prizes?" "That would never do," his mother had pointed out. "Prizes are supposed to glitter."

And the achievement wasn't supposed to tarnish. It was always supposed to make you feel good. Something else went click inside Alec. "I think you want me to win the race for you — not for me!"

"I want you to win it for both of us. Come on now! You can do it!"

"No," said Alec. "I can't."

He hung up. The click that had happened while he was talking to his grandfather must have started a feeling-cross cycle. Why wouldn't everyone let him alone! Why did his grandfather have to act that way — as if Alec were hurting him by letting him down? He wondered if Old Lob had ever realized how hurt Alec had been when he never built the boat he'd promised. That was being let down in a big way.

Alec went out on the front porch again. Maybe there would be a breeze blowing across the bay that would skim over the cove and still be strong enough to flutter through the screens. There wasn't. The bay looked like a gigantic puddle of melted glass as the sun highlighted its surface. Boats searched for a breath of air but their sails drooped. A few powerboats sped across the sea, trying to make their own breeze. People stood up in them, letting their hair stream out and hoping for a shiver of spray to cool them off.

Alec was sweating. He stripped off his T-shirt, and when he saw it was the one that declared ROW FOR IT, he threw it on the floor in a corner.

"Yah, Alec." Stomper opened the screen door and stuck his head in.

"Hi."

"Seen the *Enterprise?*"

"Not yet. The paper boy's late."

"I picked one up when I was in Rowbery. My mom's got it now. My picture's on the front page. It says "Gilbert R. Gates, hero of boat accident at Flounder Cove."

"Why don't they say Stomper?"

"Mom told them to say Gilbert R. She hates Stomper. So they got it right. They got your name wrong though. You're Alexandra Bott."

Alec groaned. It was bad enough to be written up as a victim, a kind of helpless dummy that was hauled about. But to turn his name into a girl's? And *Bott?*

He could imagine his father's cry of disgust. "No human ever proofreads the *Enterprise* now! They just let computers set type any old way. How do they expect kids to learn to spell and read when they are destroying the written word before our eyes!" His father said that at least once a week while he was reading the paper.

Stomper went on. "I got interviewed, too. Of course it's only a sidebar —"

"A what?"

"The reporter said that's a little piece that goes along beside a main story. The big story is looking for the boat that ran you down and the boat-owners' complaints about conditions at Flounder Cove. So the reporter said I'm local color."

"Great. I'll read about it."

"Anyway — I'm taking *Flashdance* out for a run over to the lighthouse and back. There's only one more day to the trial heats. When I get back, you can take *Flashdance* out for a workout, if you want. I'll leave the oars in Salty's shed."

"I'm still not going to race."

"Too bad. I saw the trophy today at the Chamber of Commerce. It's humungous. About three feet high and a gold rowboat on top with a guy in it rowing. It's super."

"Great. I hope you win it."

"I'm going to. Well — you know where the oars are if you change your mind."

During the next half-hour, Alec sat and watched Stomper carry the oars onto the dock, bum a ride out to *Flashdance* with a little kid in a plastic boat, loose the mooring, work his way through the anchored boats and out the gap, settle to the oars, and head into the brilliant afternoon light. The sun touched Stomper's figure and the *Flashdance*, highlighting the edges of their shapes with gold that flashed with each motion of the oars. The boy and the boat glittered like a trophy. Alec shut his eyes. There was another click and he knew he had never in his life been so unhappy, so thoroughly and totally miserable.

That was how his father found him, hunched into his unhappiness.

Mr. Mott tugged off his clothes. It was so hot he didn't seem to care that he stood on the front porch in his Jockey shorts. He swung first one foot and then the other and wiggled his toes, airing them. Alec didn't even bother to say "Pee-yew!" and hold his nose the way he would have when he was younger.

His father looked at him as if he'd been expecting Alec to do that. To do something. Not just to sit there congealed into misery.

"I'm too hot," said Mr. Mott. "It's really got to me today."

"Take a shower."

"Not even a shower will do it. Where's your mother? And Jeannie?"

"Swimming. Beyond the sea wall."

"How about it? I'll put my trunks on and we'll go join them and see how cool it is by the water."

"No thanks."

"What have you been doing today?"

"Nothing much."

"I think you mean, just plain *nothing*. Right?"

"Right."

His father sat down, thrumming his fingers on the arms of the wicker chair. There was another click inside Alec and he suddenly felt defensive. "Well — even if I was going to race, I don't have a boat to work out in. And I just don't feel like going out on the water anyway. You ought to understand that better than anyone else."

"Oh, I do! And I'm not going to let a mistake I made years ago happen again. It doesn't matter to me whether you race or not, but it does matter that you get back on your horse as soon after you're thrown as possible."

Mr. Mott went into the house, and Alec wondered what horses and being thrown had to do with racing and his father's mistakes. His father made a phone call. Then he went upstairs and came back wearing his running shorts. But he didn't have on his Nikes. He was wearing flip-flops.

"That was an interesting conversation I just had with Ezra Elliott. First, he'll have *Miss L.* fixed up and bring her back to Flounder Cove tomorrow morning. Second, he says Stomper came by his workshop to see how long the *Miss L.* would be laid up. He told Ezra he'd let you work out with *Flashdance* today if you felt like it."

"I know. He told me. He's out in the boat now."

Mr. Mott looked over at the cove. "Actually he's just rowing in the gap. Come on, Alec. I want you to take me out in the *Flashdance* and row me around to where your mother and Jeannie are on the rocks."

"But you —"

"Don't argue. We'll just do it."

From the jetty, they hailed Stomper and he rowed in to the dock.

"How's the weather out there? Cooler?" Mr. Mott asked.

"Not much." Stomper glistened with sweat. "Just tie her up on the mooring and put the oars in Salty's shed when you're through. Have a good row."

"Thanks," said Mr. Mott. "Okay, Alec. I'll get in first." The boat bobbed briskly as he stepped in, caught his balance, and settled onto the stern seat. Alec hesitated. Even that little unsteadiness on the dinghy's part reminded him of how quickly the *Miss L.* had been flipped. His legs began to feel shaky, as if the bones had been replaced again by those shifting plastic peanuts.

"Alec — just do it." His father didn't say, "If I can do it, you can." But he knew that was the hook his father was luring him by.

Alec hopped in and sat down in a hurry. The boat swung and banged the dock. "Hey!" yelled Stomper, who lingered on the gangway. "Don't wreck my boat!"

Alec didn't answer. He reached over and shoved *Flashdance* away from the dock. They drifted as he pushed the oars out in the oarlocks. Someone in the cove started up a motor with a spewing of bluish exhaust fumes and a series of rattling explosions. Alec tensed.

"Shall I coach?" asked his father. "I can't be the coxswain. I'm too big and I'm in the wrong end of the boat."

"I'm not working out."

"I know. I just meant for you to put those oars in and start controlling the boat. Don't let yourself be spooked by the sound of that motor. Just start rowing."

Slowly Alec dipped the oars and pushed the *Flashdance* toward the gap. After the first few strokes, his tenseness eased up. The rhythm of dip, pull, and lift came back. The powerboat was throttled down and waited its turn to pass out through the breakwater after Alec was safely through.

Once outside the cove the dinghy rose and fell over a long slow swell. "You want me to row past where Mum is?" Alec looked over his shoulder to choose his path through the pot buoys. "What'll we do? Both yell, 'Hey, look at me'?"

"Something like that. Just stay about a hundred feet offshore."

Alec realized it was his father who was tense now, as he rowed out around Salty's trap net and then came in closer to the rocks. They could see Mrs. Mott reading a paperback and Jeannie paddling about in a tide pool. Christopher Elvis was lying on his back, sporting a pair of sunglasses.

"Hey!" Alec called.

Mrs. Mott stood up, smiling and waving. "Wonderful! I wish I had my camera!"

"This is close enough," said Mr. Mott. "You take the boat in." Very quickly Alec's father stood up on the stern seat and dove off. It wasn't a great dive and it set the *Flashdance* to rocking like a horse on a merry-go-round. Right up and right down! Alec sat there, riding out the motion, oars poised, watching his father swimming to the shore. His crawl stroke was abrupt and choppy, and Alec was sure he could hear each gasp of breath his father took as he turned his face in and out of the water. He let the *Flashdance* drift, while his mother walked to the edge of the rocks and told his father where to swim in through the seaweed. She gave him her hand and pulled him safely ashore. Mr. Mott stood up and waved at Alec.

"That's one way to get cool."

"Right," said Alec. "You're cool."

He rowed back to the cove, secured *Flashdance,* bummed a ride to the dock with Pete, and left the oars in Salty's shed. Then he went over to where Nancy Wentworth was sunning on the jetty in her orange bikini. "Want to swim?"

"Sure."

It was high tide, so they each took a couple of running steps and flung themselves out over the edge of the jetty, jumping, to come down feet first in a space temporarily empty of boats. As Alec's head sank briefly under the surface and bubbles whizzed up around him from his splash and he began paddling up for air, he felt one more click. He wasn't afraid anymore.

He was in motion again. It was the most natural thing in the world to be rolling around in the water, feeling it buoy him up, feeling the salt tingling his eyes and his nose, feeling how good it was to stretch out and swim. And he knew that tomorrow when the *Miss L.* came back he'd be ready to get in her and row and row and row.

14

On Friday morning Alec waited at Flounder Cove for Grover Tarr to come with his pickup truck and drive him, along with the *Miss L.*, over to Rowbery. Miss Longley had arranged it. Alec looked around for Stomper and found that there were no boats at the Gateses' mooring. "Stomper gone already?" he asked Salty.

"Early this morning. The powerboat's towing *Flash-dance* around to Rowbery, and the Gateses are letting the Race Committee use the big boat for something or other. Stomper said to tell you he was through being nice. He's out to beat the stuffing out of you."

"I'll bet he didn't say stuffing."

"You're right. He didn't."

"Hey, Alec!" Pirate Pete sat in his boat, straightening out a tangle of rope. "I can't get over for the trials today, but I'll sure be there Sunday. Go for it. Good luck."

"Thanks." Alec heard Grover Tarr's truck rattling onto the jetty. The two of them hoisted the *Miss L.* into the truck. Alec climbed into the cab. As Mr. Tarr turned the ignition key and started the motor with a click and a whir, Alec felt as if his mind did the same to his body. *Click.* This was it! *Whirr-rr-rr.* He was off to the races. To make his best try. His *personal best,* as the sports announcers on TV liked to call it.

The Motts waved at him from the front porch as the truck went by. They had invited Miss Longley to ride over with them in time to find a picnic spot on the Esplanade. Alec's father was even taking the day off from his office.

Alec found his grandfather waiting for him at the Public Landing in Rowbery, where entrants for the races were picking up their T-shirts and their racing numbers and putting their boats in the water.

"I told you you didn't really want to drop out of the race," said Old Lob. "You'll do just fine. You'll have all these other fellows wearing the seats out of their pants, trying to keep up with you."

Alec wished his grandfather wasn't quite so loud about it, especially when he was reminding his friends that his grandson already had one trophy for rowing. But it did help to have Old Lob fasten the large number 8 on the back of Alec's T-shirt. The Chamber of Commerce had added a bit more advertising to the shirt this year. It now read ROW FOR IT IN ROWBERY. Underneath the letters was a pair of crossed oars. The color was a raw red. With sunshine and seawater, it should fade well, so Alec thought at least the shirt would be worth his making the effort.

"If I win, I win," he said to his grandfather. "If I don't, I don't. But I'll try."

"You'll win." His grandfather had no doubt about it.

Alec found there would be four dinghies on the course at the same time. There were now twelve boats entered in his class so there would be three heats. The winners of each heat would be the finalists on Sunday. He didn't see Stomper, so he asked the official on the dock what Stomper's number was.

"Gates. Gates, Gilbert. He's number 3. So he's in the first heat. They're lining up at the starting line now. Got your boat in?"

"Right over there."

"Okay. You're in the second heat. Once they start, you get out to the starting line and wait there for your turn."

Old Lob was full of last-minute advice. He made Alec look through binoculars at the points on the course where the markers were. They were big Day-Glo orange floats with flags of the same eye-grabbing color. Alec focused the glasses on the four boats spaced out at the starting line. Stomper was adjusting the sweatband on his forehead. That was a smart idea! You didn't want to take your hands off the oars even to wipe the sweat out of your eyes.

"That's the Gateses' powerboat anchored out there," his grandfather said. "Gates loaned the boat to the committee and one of the course judges is stationed in it. He's a friend of mine. He's honest. He won't give an advantage to the Gates boy. And he wouldn't give you one, either. You just go for it, Alec, and you'll make it."

"I know. Do me a favor? If I win my heat so I race

132

Sunday, will you buy a sweatband for me at the Sports Shop? I'll pay you back."

"No need to pay me. It'll be my pleasure."

The sound of a gun echoed in the harbor. With a flashing of oars the four boats crossed the starting line. "That Chamber of Commerce is getting more like a yacht club every year," objected Old Lob. "It used to be somebody counted one-two-three-GO! Now they use a gun just like the yacht races."

Alec didn't want to stand about talking anymore. He stepped into the *Miss L.*, settled himself into place, unshipped the oars, and slowly rowed out into the harbor. When he came near the starting line, he turned the boat around so he could watch the heat in progress without having to peer over his shoulder. It didn't seem to be much of a contest. One dinghy, which looked as if it was shaped to float on a peaceful pond, skittered at each tap of a wave, and the boy in it had trouble staying on a straight line toward his next marker. Another fellow was rowing so fast he'd never be able to keep it up, and he wasn't checking his direction. He'd be wide around the mark. Two boats were rounding the halfway flag, with Stomper and *Flashdance* some ten feet ahead. Stomper kept the same distance all the way to the finish line.

"Nothing to it!" he called to Alec. "There's some chop out there where you cross the harbor channel — but that's the only place. I'm only telling you that so you'll win this heat and I can beat you in the finals."

Alec swung the *Miss L.* into position. The official had an electronic bullhorn and he was giving them instructions. Wait for the starting gun. They'd be called back if there was a false start. Go to the outside of each course buoy. Good luck. May the best boat win.

Alec had time to look at the competition. You could call them skiffs, rowboats, prams, or dinghies. It didn't seem to matter much. They were all about the same length. There was some variation in the width and the curve of the sides and depth of the bottom. Suddenly Alec thought of the metal junk he'd told Salty he'd dump. It had been in the stern seat when he capsized. It could have been one of the reasons the bow went up and over so quickly — because of the extra weight in the stern.

Alec leaned forward and unlatched the hook on the seat lid and flipped it open. There was the junk. Ezra Elliott had been so busy mending the bow in a rush, he hadn't bothered to check out the stern.

"Wait!" Alec waved at the official. "I'm not ready!" The man looked puzzled and even more so as Alec began throwing junk into the water. He conferred with another official and then asked over the bullhorn, "Is anyone else carrying any weight they want to get rid of?"

One boy even threw out a plastic bailing jug that went spinning off on the tide.

"All set?"

There were no more problems. Each boy had his oars poised, and at the gun, off they went. Alec had checked his course to the first marker by taking a heading on the tower of Rowbery City Hall. He kept his eyes on that and was sure he'd come out close to the right of the buoy for a quick turn. But the boy to his left was crowding him. He'd either have to pull ahead of him or be shoved farther out than he wanted to be. Alec concentrated on getting ahead. His plan worked and by the time he rounded the halfway flag, there was one boat ahead of him and the other two were far enough behind that they would be no threat. Here was the rippling chop of the tide in the channel that Stomper mentioned. Alec gripped the oars tight, shortened the timing of his strokes, and kept the *Miss L.* from being pushed about. He gained on the first boat, took the third turn only a second or so behind it, and pulled hard. He could hear some yelling and cheering from people watching from their boats around the harbor. He knew his grandfather and his father and his mother and Miss Longley and Jeannie and Christopher Elvis would be cheering, too. Nancy had told him she would be cheering for Stomper. Alec hoped, if she'd heard he was racing after all, she'd be there now, yelling for him. He leaned into the pattern and felt the impulse to make stronger pulls flow from his thighs to his back to his shoulders and down his arms to his fingers. His head sang: lean, stroke, PULL, lift. Lean, stroke, PULL, lift. He skimmed past the other boat. Lean, stroke, PULL-LL, lift. He was over the finish line first by a few seconds.

Boat horns and whistles tooted. It had been a good race. Something for the spectators to cheer about.

Alec let his grip loosen on the oars. In these last few pulls he'd felt as if his hands were burning. He hoped his calluses held and he hadn't started any new blisters. He wished the final race was right away. A zillion things could happen between now and Sunday.

When he tied up the *Miss L.* at the Public Landing, his grandfather was there to slap him on the shoulder. "See? I told you you'd do it. Let's go down the Esplanade and find the folks."

"And the drinks!" Alec was thirsty.

By the time they had walked to where the Esplanade fronted the harbor, the boats in the last heat were on the third leg of the course. It was a tight race, with three boats finishing strongly, and from where Alec stood, it looked like a two-way tie. It must have looked like that to the judges, too, because when the announcement came of the boats to race in the Sunday finals, four numbers were given: boats 3, 8, 9, and 12.

Alec had particularly noticed the fellow who was number 12. "Do you know his name?"

"That's Tony Brosnan. I checked out his age, he seems so big — like he should be in the Junior Varsity Oarsmen class," Old Lob said. "But he just makes it in your class. Three weeks from now and he'd be thirteen and have to compete with fellows bigger than he is. But you can beat Stomper, can't you? And he's bigger than you."

"I don't know. We never finished the race we were having. That's when I got capsized."

"Have they found the *Old-Man-of-the-Sea* yet?"

"No. Dad thinks maybe the man heard the Coast Guard is looking for his boat. Maybe he just kept on heading north and he'll lie low way up the Maine coast until the fuss dies down. But he won't dare to come back to Flounder Cove."

They found the Motts and Miss Longley and settled down on the grass to have their picnic and watch the heats for the Junior Varsity Oarsmen race. The trials for the Senior Varsity Oarsmen and the International Dory races would be held on Saturday.

When Jeannie announced that Christopher Elvis wanted a balloon, Mr. Mott gave her a dollar and said, "Get him two. One for each hand."

"And tie the balloons right on," Alec urged. "He'll take off and fly away."

"Creep-o," said Jeannie.

She went along the Esplanade walk, pushing Christopher Elvis, who was strapped into her old stroller. She came back with one purple balloon tied onto Christopher Elvis's wrist.

"What's the matter?" Alec asked. "Were you really afraid he'd take off?"

"No. Dad only gave me a dollar. I couldn't get two balloons. They're a dollar each."

"Good heavens!" said Miss Longley. "Balloons used to be a nickel apiece."

"Blown up with helium?" asked Mrs. Mott.

"No," said Old Lob. "Blown up with good old human hot air." He and Miss Longley sat on a bench and remembered long-forgotten delights — from wax harmonicas that you could chew ("Ghastly for your health!" said Mrs. Mott) to ice skates that clamped onto your shoes. ("No wonder people couldn't spin and jump on skates the way they do now," said Mr. Mott.) Alec heard it all going on around him. He heard the man with the spicy hot dogs talking up his trade, and kids trying to keep a Frisbee game going without interference from dogs or cops.

When Mrs. Mott suggested it was time to go home, Alec asked, "Is it safe to leave the *Miss L.* tied up till Sunday at the Public Landing?"

"I'll keep an eye on her," Old Lob promised.

"And pick up a sweatband for me?"

"Don't worry. I'll take care of everything."

15

It seemed to Alec that Saturday drawled by — like a record put on the player at too low a speed. Or that his life had gone into an overtime period, but no one could yet blow an official whistle to get the play under way.

Nothing but the usual confusion of weekend sailors was going on at the cove. Stomper and his family were spending the weekend in Rowbery Harbor, since their powerboat had a cabin that slept four. Alec suggested driving to Rowbery Saturday afternoon so he could check on his grandfather's checking on the *Miss L.* and getting him a sweatband. But both his mother and father had other things to do. Scooty, when Alec phoned him, had to go out of town to a cousin's wedding. He wouldn't, to his disgust, get to try the greasy pole contest.

Everyone was up early on Sunday. The Pee Wee finals began in the morning at ten, with the Junior Rowers finals to start at eleven. Alec ate a breakfast of bananas and milk and brown sugar on cereal and finished off with two English muffins with peanut butter and jelly. Before eight o'clock. At eight-thirty he was still in the kitchen, bothering his mother about putting their picnic together.

"I'm waiting for the eggs to hard-boil," she told him. "If you're so impatient, go sit in the car."

"Jeannie's there. She's got Christopher Elvis strapped into the car seat already."

"Then help me. Don't hinder me."

She gave him the bread and the mayonnaise and the lettuce and the cold cuts and told him to start organizing the sandwiches. Miss Longley would join them again and she was bringing the cold drinks and the dessert.

"Nervous?" Mrs. Mott asked when she noticed Alec putting mayonnaise on both sides of a piece of bread.

"No. Yes. What do you expect me to be!"

"Nervous. Dumb question."

"I'm not nervous about whether I win or not. But I'm nervous about grandfather. What will happen to him if I don't win? He's got his heart set on it and he's so sure I will he's been boasting to all his friends."

"And you're being more realistic about it? That makes sense, Alec. You're not exactly the biggest boy in your race."

Alec was glad his mother said it that way — much more tactful than saying, "You're the smallest boy in your race."

"Right."

"How your grandfather takes it isn't your problem. It's his. He's a dear man, but we all know he can be

140

difficult. Anyway, don't worry about him. Just do the best you can and we'll all be proud of you."

Alec kept her words in mind as his father let him out of the car at the Rowbery Public Landing and then helped him untie the oars from the roof rack. Alec hadn't dared leave them in the dinghy.

The family drove off, their good-luck cries ringing in his ears. Alec felt quite alone, in spite of the confusion around the landing. Once he got into the *Miss L.*, though, he knew he wouldn't feel alone. She had become not just the dinghy he was racing, but a trusted friend. They'd been through so much together. He'd almost forgotten that she wasn't *his* boat — that she belonged to Miss Longley and was only on loan for the summer.

He didn't see his grandfather in the crowd and that surprised him — and worried him. Old Lob had promised to check on the *Miss L.* and to bring him a sweatband. He'd need one, as it was already a hot morning for the first weekend of September. The sun seemed to cast its light down so heavily you felt its solid heat encasing you, and it took work to make yourself move through it.

Alec made his way along a gangway to the float where some of the boats entered in the races were tied. There was the *Miss L.* He hopped into her and checked her out. She didn't need bailing. The oarlocks rotated easily. There was nothing inside the stern seat but a plastic bailer and an extra rope. His mother had basted his number onto the back of his T-shirt, so he didn't have to worry about pins working loose and stabbing him.

"Alec! I took good care of the *Miss L.* for you!" Old Lob stood on the float. "Even came down at midnight after that thunderstorm to see she was safe. Bailed her out for you early this morning."

"Thanks! Where's the sweatband?"

Old Lob ducked his head. "I don't think you'll need one. They get to binding your forehead something fierce. Like an iron headache. And itchy! You'd be wanting to let go of the oars and push it up and scratch all the time."

"You didn't get one, did you!" Alec knew he should have gone to Rowbery yesterday and done the errand himself.

"Well now, I was so busy keeping an eye on your boat with all the crowds coming and going yesterday I didn't get around to it. And this morning — it's Sunday and the Sports Shop is closed. But what's a little sweat in your eyes, Alec? It's your *hands* you don't want sweaty. You don't want them to slip on the oars."

"I really wanted a sweatband. It could really help."

His grandfather stuck his hands in his pants pockets. "Look!" He pulled out a much-folded, but clean, blue bandanna. "What about this?" He snapped it diagonally into a roll. "Let me tie this around your head."

"I don't know." Alec was doubtful. "What if it slipped?"

"It won't. I can tie it so you'll be comfortable but it will be good and tight. Don't worry!"

Old Lob made Alec get out of the boat and stand

142

on the float while he tied the bandanna around his head. He caught some of Alec's hair in the knot.

"Yike!"

"Sorry. You need a haircut."

Old Lob tied it again. Alec pushed it more comfortably onto his forehead.

"Junior Rowers! Attention — Junior Rowers!" The announcement vibrated over the bullhorn. "Get out to the starting line. You have twenty minutes until your race."

"You'll do great," Old Lob pronounced. "You'll have a great pair of trophies."

"Maybe."

"No — you'll do it," his grandfather insisted. Alec remembered his grandfather's credo: Think Big. And his mother's: Think Positive. He remembered how he'd concentrated so hard on holding a winning raffle ticket.

And then he'd won Christopher Elvis.

Maybe it was best just to row and think about how and where he was rowing.

He pushed off from the float and followed numbers 9 and 12, who were already on the way. The course was still set out as it had been for the trial heats. His headings would be the same. There was no wind like the one that had skipped about the harbor on Friday. The ocean rose and fell slowly, as if it, too, were panting from the heat.

Alec saw Stomper already by the starting line. The Gates family were on their powerboat. He noticed the Merrills' sailboat, the *Windward HoHo IV*, anchored a little farther on. Scooty and his mother and father were all waving and making applauding gestures. For a start Scooty seemed to be cheering for both Stomper and Alec.

An official came by holding a cap with slips of paper in it. Each boy drew for his position at the start. Alec and Stomper drew places next to each other.

While they paddled about, getting into position, Alec thought he ought to be a good sport and wish Stomper well. Like the Olympic runners in *Chariots of Fire* who shook hands and wished each other luck before the race. After all, he owed Stomper a lot. Maybe even his life. He should at least wish him well.

Alec called, "Hey, Stomper! Here's —"

But his words were lost under Stomper's growl of greeting. "Shut up, creep, and keep out of my way."

It looked as if he was back to being the old Stomper. Alec wondered if the boy who'd pulled him in with an oar and had offered him the use of *Flashdance* had been real or only a spirit that had briefly visited Stomper's body. But he saw Stomper grin. Who knew what went on in Stomper's head? Alec didn't have time to worry about it.

"Get set!" The voice on the bullhorn crackled and boomed.

Alec braced his feet, flexed his fingers, gripped the oars, and at the *WHOMP* of the gun, pulled out onto the glaring water. He tried not to look at what was happening with the other boats or be disturbed by the rasp of a pair of oarlocks that were being worked at a faster pace than his. But he was aware they were all crowding each other, getting too close as they headed for the first marker. It took some strategy to think out the race as they went along. If the rowboats ended up too close it could be like a jousting tournament, with oars instead of lances clashing at each other.

Alec glanced over his shoulder. Stomper and Tony seemed to be jockeying for the closest turn, and Tony suddenly shipped one oar and slipped around the marker so tightly that he escaped from Stomper's effort to cut him off. One of Stomper's oars came down with a bang on the stern of Tony's boat. The oar didn't break and Stomper soon caught his old rhythm. Alec shot the *Miss L.* around right behind them, and the fourth boat, which had gone wider to avoid the traffic jam, was rocking a bit in the wakes of the other boats.

By the halfway marker Tony had strayed off his course just enough so Stomper was first around the mark. Alec made it a close third and the last dinghy was definitely falling behind. It looked as if the boy rowing it had developed a cramp.

This was the leg of the course where the chop had been so strong before and Alec had planned to put his biggest effort into holding his course — pulling stronger on one oar than the other. He'd done a lot of that in his training. He didn't waver at all. He came up to the third marker close behind Tony, who was soon pushing Stomper into a furious contest.

As they began this last leg back into the main part of the harbor, Alec could hear the cheering from the crowds on the Headlands and the Esplanade, and from the people on boats anchored along the piers and the shore. "GO FOR IT! ROW FOR IT!" kept ringing out, beginning in different places, carried along by different groups, mounting skyward like the old round, "Row, Row, Row Your Boat," declaimed by a chorus of thousands. The noise seemed to strike the brassy sky like clashing cymbals. Yet Alec felt quite alone at the heart of the noise.

He felt the sweat dribbling down his back, seeping under his hands — and he felt the knot in the bandanna loosening. It was beginning to slip. He shook his head, hoping to fling the whole thing off. But the bandanna was just loosening and loosening.

Alec was afraid the thing would slip over his eyes and he'd be blindfolded. He knew it! Had his grandfather ever come through with anything that he'd promised or that worked the way he said it would!

If Alec reached up to pull the bandanna off, he could lose an oar. As it was, he lost his concentration. He caught a crab, something he hadn't done since the first day he'd taken the *Miss L.* out. Not even the splash of cold water made him feel better. The bandanna fell over his eyes and he couldn't see. He had to let go of the oar and pull at it, yanking it fiercely down around his neck. He finally caught the oar again as it began slipping out of the oarlock. He had to pull hard to keep the boat on course.

Those awkward seconds cost him. He couldn't catch Stomper or Tony now. Alec became aware of the painful stitch in his side, the ache in his shoulders, the trembling in his legs, and yet his arms and his back and his hands wouldn't give up. Lean, pull, lift. LEAN, PULL, LIFT. Maybe ten more times. Now nine! Now eight!

He heard the whistles and horns let loose. Either Tony or Stomper had won. Five, four, perhaps. *Lean, pull, lift* — could he manage to do it three more times? One more big effort. And again, one more.

He looked to the side and saw the *Miss L.* was gliding beyond the marker. He'd finished the race. He could quit. He heaved the oars in, leaned over trying to catch his breath and ease the stitch in his side, and let the boat drift.

The official announced over the bullhorn, "Winner of the Junior Rowers trophy is Tony Brosnan. Second is Gil Gates. Third is Alec Mott. And now hear this: All three boys beat the old course record — and all three of them finished within ninety seconds of each other. Congratulations to all three winners."

"Hey Alec!" Stomper was still breathing hard. "At least you finished."

Alec glared at Stomper. He started to say, "If that bandanna hadn't slipped, I could have beaten you!" But maybe he would have and maybe he wouldn't have. That was something that could never be proved.

"Not bad for a little guy," Stomper went on.

"If you're so much bigger, you should have beaten me by more than sixty seconds, Stomper."

"Gil," corrected Stomper. "Didn't you hear? Gil Gates."

Gil? Well, maybe. Stomper as a name was so thoroughly stamped onto Alec's tongue, it would be hard to change.

Alec saw Stomper row off toward the Gateses' boat. On the way in to the landing, Alec passed Pirate Pete, whose craft sat low in the water, as he'd loaded not only Salty but quite a few of the other lobstermen and fishermen from the cove on board. They all cheered and yelled, "Way to go, Alec! You did good!" Alec grinned. It felt good to be recognized and cheered by people who weren't even related to him.

At the landing Alec had to wait a bit to tie up. He looked for his grandfather on the dock and wondered how Old Lob would greet him. The bandanna still hung where he'd wrenched it down around his neck.

Alec hadn't won the gorgeously gilded trophy. He didn't even know what the third prize was. A framed certificate? A ribbon? He didn't really care. But he had the feeling his grandfather was still adjusting to the results: his grandson had come in third — not first. That perhaps he was avoiding his old pals to whom he'd done a lot of boasting that his grandson would win oars down. And perhaps he was still figuring out what to say to Alec, thinking that losing the race would make him really miserable.

But it didn't. Really miserable had been how Alec had felt several days ago, when he was uncertain and unhappy. Right now, except for the stitch that still caught at his side and the worn-out feeling that naturally followed such a lavish use of energy, Alec felt fine. He wasn't even mad about the bandanna anymore. Maybe that was what was keeping his grandfather away; he figured Alec would be upset because the bandanna slipped at a crucial moment. Alec looked about for Old Lob.

As he stepped off the dock, Nancy met him. She was carrying so many balloons they looked like a swarm.

"Hi, Alec! Here! I'm ballooning you." She handed a great bunch to him. "Don't look so surprised. Didn't you know people get ballooned now — for birthdays and celebrations? It's special."

"Wow! It sure is!" Alec smiled up at the balloons bobbing over his head. They made him feel giddy. So did Nancy's giving them to him. "Neat-o. Thanks."

"Now I have to find Stomper. The other bunch is for him. See you around the cove."

Alec felt a little silly, standing there holding a pair of oars with one hand and a bunch of balloons with the other. But not *that* silly. The thought that Nancy gave him a special honor buoyed him up. Now everything was fine except for his grandfather. Alec went searching for him.

Old Lob was in the parking lot above the Public Landing, making a hassle out of putting his binoculars back in their case.

"Hi! Could you take these for a minute?" Alec handed him the oars. Then he tied the web of balloon string to a belt loop on his cut-offs. After all, only little kids had balloons tied to their wrists. "Did you get a good look at the race?"

"Yes, I did. Damn that bandanna. I knew you didn't need to bother with a sweatband."

"Here —" Alec pulled the bandanna around and untied the already loosened knot. "I did need it. Feel how wet it is. It really did keep the sweat out of my eyes."

"Well, you keep it. I don't want it," said Old Lob, disowning the whole affair. "You were certainly right in there. You couldn't have been closer behind than you were."

A friend of Old Lob's came by. "Congratulations, Alec. That was a real tight race. A fine race, and you had some really big competition."

"Thanks," said Alec.

"He did all right, didn't he!" said Old Lob. "Well, that's my grandson." He shouldered the oars and they set off for the Esplanade to find the Motts.

Old Lob began to feel better about the race after several more of his pals congratulated Alec as they walked along. Even if Alec's grandfather had to discard his Think Big or Think First for Think Smaller, Think Third, he was on his way again to Think Positive.

When they caught up with the family, Old Lob said, "If Alec's foolish bandanna I told him he didn't need hadn't slipped, he'd have won that race."

Alec and his mother looked at each other. Then they laughed. Old Lob would always be Old Lob — and they both loved him.

Jeannie made Christopher Elvis's hands clap and said in a baby voice, "Way to go, Alec." In her own voice she asked, "What's with the balloons? Did you get them for me?"

"No. I got ballooned by a friend. I'm taking them home. But I'll tie them on Christopher Elvis's stroller for now."

"Oh no you won't! They'd fly off with him."

Alec pulled the balloons down and felt their surge upward with a big tug as he let up the strings. Maybe Jeannie was right. He tied the web to his mother's folding chair. "But don't get up!"

"I won't let them take off," she promised. "Alec, what a good race! You really thought it out. I watched the way you were always aware of getting crowded or jammed and the way you really zipped around the buoys. You couldn't have done that better."

"When you get to college, you'll be a great man at crew!" said Mr. Mott. "You kept up a fast, strong sweep until you were across the finish line."

"What do you get for being third?" Jeannie asked.

"I don't know. Nobody seemed to be giving out prizes after the race."

"Or taking pictures." Old Lob sounded as if he'd expected to be photographed for the newspaper as his winning grandson's coach. "But you'll find out at four o'clock. There's the stand for the mayor and the winners over there. The high school band will play and there'll be speeches."

Alec looked across the grass to the middle of the Esplanade, where a wooden platform had been built. It was just like the Olympics: there were three stands on the platform, each a different height. If only Alec had come in first, he'd be on the tallest one — and that would make him even a bit taller than Stomper or

151

Tony as they stood on lower ones. It didn't seem fair that the shortest boy had to stand on the lowest place. But — that's the way it is, Alec had to remind himself. And it would be exciting to be one of the three standing there, hearing the band play and the mayor make his speech, and receiving the prize from the president of the Chamber of Commerce.

"I can tell you what the third prize is," said Miss Longley. "It's a plaque. A metal plaque that says *Third Prize — Junior Rowers — Rowbery Race Week — 1986.* It's on exhibit beyond the platform."

"We can put it up in the living room if you like," said Mrs. Mott.

"Maybe," said Alec.

"I really would like to stay for the award ceremony," said Miss Longley, "but I do have to be back in Annisconset in an hour." She had driven herself over that day so she wouldn't upset the Motts' afternoon by leaving early. "It's been a great pleasure for me to watch the races and picnic with you Friday and today. This summer has been much more fun than I've had in quite a few years. Our adventure on the island, Alec, and becoming reacquainted with Flounder Cove and all that goes on there. But I was around the cove enough to realize that taking care of a boat year-round is a responsibility I don't need to add to my life now. So I wonder, Alec, if you'd be kind enough to accept a — well, a first prize — from me. If only a dinghy had a set of keys like a car or a powerboat, I could hand you the keys. I can't do that, so I'll transfer ownership of the *Miss L.* from me to you with an official handshake."

Miss Longley held out her hand. Alec put his hand in hers and they shook solemnly.

"You've really earned it," she said. "Now — have fun and enjoy her. The *Miss L.* is all yours."

"Thanks! THANKS!"

Alec felt as breathless as he'd felt at the Sea Fest, waiting for the winning raffle ticket to be drawn. It was as if the weeks of tough training for the race had hardly happened and he'd just won the raffle. What had seemed so unfair at the time had turned out all right. This time it was really fair. He'd won it on his own.